Mr. Prickles and

His Holiday Adventure

Mr. Prickles and His Holiday Adventure

by

Leia Kirschner

Emerald Eyes Publishing
Aurora, IL

Visit our website at www.emeraldeyespublishing.com

LCCN: 2021922889
ISBN: 978-1-7374845-6-1

Illustrations by Jennifer Hansen

Printed in the U.S.A.

For all our little pet friends who like to go on adventures.

Chapter 1

Everything on the end block of Waterbury Street was as normal as it could be for a breezy autumn afternoon. No different than any other street block. There was a woman walking her dog on the sidewalk, a delivery man setting packages on doorsteps, and a school bus dropping off an eager group of fourth-graders as they returned home from school. One student, however, appeared to be more eager to get home than the rest. She was so antsy that she even forgot to close the door once inside.

"Did the package come?!" asked Lilly, whose dad was still busy working in his at-home office.

"No. Sorry, sweetie. It hasn't come yet."

"Oh," she said with noticeable disappointment. "I saw the delivery truck outside and thought it came."

"Hmm. It must've been for the house next door. No one has rung the bell all day."

"Can't you call the post office people to ask where it is?" she asked. "Maybe it got lost. We've been waiting for days, and I'm worried that something might've happened to it."

"I'm sure it didn't get lost," dad reassured her. "The email said it was on its way, but with it being the week after Black Friday, I've got a feeling that we might have to wait a couple days extra."

"A couple days? But a couple days is such a long time away."

"Geez, kiddo! I've never seen you this anxious about shipping before. Maybe next time we should click on the next-day delivery option. That way, they'll know how important it is and ship it here as fast as they can," he said with a smirk.

"It isn't for me though," she reminded him. "It's for Mr. Prickles, remember?"

"Oh yeah, that's right. Sorry, I forgot. Well, tell Mr. Prickles that he might have to wait a little bit longer, but I'll be sure to let him know as soon as it arrives, okay?"

"You can't tell him!" she stressed. "It's supposed to be a surprise!"

"Oh, I'm sorry. Alright, I'll tell *you* when it comes, okay?"

"Okay."

As Lilly stood there watching her dad work, a curious thought suddenly entered her mind.

"Dad, why is it you get to work from home, but mom still has to leave home for work?"

He stopped what he was doing, smiled, and turned around to answer her question.

"Well, remember a couple of years ago when a lot of people were scared of getting sick, and the government made everyone stay home and wear masks if they went out?"

Lilly nodded her head. "Yes, I remember. I had to do everything for school at home too."

"Well, after that ended, some companies realized that things turned out better when people worked from home.

Unfortunately, that wasn't the case for everyone. Since your mom is one of the people who helps those in charge of big companies, she still has to go to an office building a few times a week. Hence, why I'm the one who has to cook dinner most nights. If I didn't, then you wouldn't be eating until nearly your bedtime."

"I wish mom could work from home like you do."

"You and me both, kiddo. You and me both."

With that said, Lilly told her dad that she was going upstairs to her room to start on her homework. He let her know to call him if she needed any help.

Once inside her room, Lilly threw her backpack onto the bed, took off her jacket, and ran straight to the little wooden house that sat beside her bed. To most people, the small box of decorated wood would've been mistaken for a less than ordinary doll house. But it wasn't a house for dolls. No, it was a home for something much more special. Laying herself on the floor next to it, Lilly peaked through the round opening in the center. As she looked inside, her eyes glanced at the sight of a slightly chubby sleeping hedgehog. Her little friend, Mr. Prickles, all rolled up into a prickly ball. He breathed ever so gently, with his quills poking all over. Lilly wanted to wake him up, just as she always wanted to do when she got home from school, but she knew it wasn't a good idea. If she did, he would've probably gotten scared, and he would've certainly been grumpy.

As Lilly learned when she first brought him home, hedgehogs weren't like people who slept at night and woke up in the morning. No, they were, in fact, the opposite. Hedgehogs were nocturnal animals, which meant they usually woke up as soon as it got dark and slept when the sun rose. It was simply the way nature made them and how they lived their lives.

"Sleep tight, Mr. Prickles. I'll see you in a few hours. Be ready for an exciting story. It's about something really neat that happened at school today."

Letting her still sleeping friend go undisturbed, Lilly picked herself up and walked over to her backpack to get her books out. She didn't really like to do the homework that the teacher gave her, but she learned to find ways to make it more enjoyable, such as listening to music or having a snack in between. Her mom would always tell her that getting good grades was one of the best things a girl could do. That being smart was almost like having a superpower.

After about an hour of sitting down at her desk, the homework was over and done with. With that out of the way, Lilly finally did the one thing that she'd been waiting to do. Turning on her handheld, she started playing her favorite video game. And what game was that? Why, Sonic the Hedgehog, of course. Yep, it's safe to say that little miss Lilly had a very deep affection for those little creatures. From the pictures framed on her wall to the plushies on her bed, it was clear she was a lover of all pets and animals. Of course, Mr. Prickles was her favorite of all. No other could beat him.

As Lilly was playing her game, she suddenly overheard a rustling sound coming from the little house in the corner. Thinking that he woke up early, she paused the game and went over to check on him. When she looked inside, however, she found that his eyes were still closed. She then noticed him twitch around in a funny way. It soon became clear to her he was having a dream. She could only wonder, what did hedgehogs even dream about?

Chapter 2

A couple of days passed, and there was still no sign of the package Lilly had been so patiently waiting for. It got to the point where her dad decided to call the company. He asked the person on the phone if it got lost, but they kept on telling him no, and that their records showed it was delivered and signed for. Lilly could hear her dad making a fuss as she stood behind him. He eventually hung up and reassured her that he was going to get to the bottom of it. Not long after, though, the sound of the garage door opening was heard. It only meant one thing.

"I think mom is home," said Lilly.

"Hmm. She must have got off early today. They're probably cutting back on hours now because of the holidays," said dad. "Well, that's good. I need a break from cooking dinner."

The door soon opened.

"Hello, everyone! I'm home," mom announced as she walked in.

Putting down her purse on the table and taking off her coat, she went up to Lilly and gave her a hug.

"Hi, mom."

"Hi, sweetie. I bet you weren't expecting me to come home so early today, were you?"

"No, I'm glad you did though."

"Heh, I bet your father is too. Since now he knows he doesn't have to cook dinner tonight. Knowing him, I probably saved you from another night of frozen pizza and canned ravioli."

"I heard that!" said dad loudly from the hallway as he headed back into his office.

"You know it's true!" she said.

Putting her attention back on Lilly, mom started asking about her day.

"So, how was school?"

"It was so much fun! Mrs. Fisher brought in her pet turtle today to show to the class. He was so cute! She said his name was Mr. Fritters. He was really shy at first and would hide his head whenever anyone went to touch him. He reminded me of Mr. Prickles a little bit."

Hearing Mr. Prickles' name mentioned caught Lilly's mom's attention.

"Oh, that reminds me, I actually have a surprise for you. Well, more for Mr. Prickles," she said, walking back to her purse.

Reaching her hand inside, she pulled out a little white cardboard box. It almost looked like a jewelry box, but slightly bigger.

"This was delivered to the office today. At first, I thought it was really strange, since I didn't remember ordering anything for work, but then I realized when we ordered your gift for Mr. Prickles, I must've accidentally had it sent to my work address."

Lilly's face instantly lit up with joy.

"Yay! Yay! Yay!" she cheered. "Dad, guess what!"

"What?" he asked from his office.

"The package finally came! Mom said that they sent it to her work!"

Dad poked his head out the doorway. "Seriously?! Wow, no wonder that guy on the phone said I was crazy."

With the box now in her hand, Lilly thanked her mom and immediately ran up to her room to show Mr. Prickles. She knew it was still a little early before his usual wake-up time, but she simply couldn't contain her excitement and decided to wake him up anyway. Plus, she knew he would be just as excited when he saw what she got him.

Entering her room and lying down next to the little hedgehog house, she slyly poked her hand inside the hole and gently nudged him to wake up.

"Hey, Mr. Prickles? I know it's early, but I have a surprise for you. Come on. Come out. I know you're going to love it."

At first, he wouldn't wake up. In fact, he actually let out a grumpy hiss. Thinking quickly, Lilly went to her desk and got the one thing she knew would wake him up. Opening the drawer, she grabbed the little jar of hedgehog treats and started shaking it. Mr. Prickles heard the ever-familiar rattling and quickly came scuttling out of his little home.

"Yeah, you like surprise treats, don't you?" she said, feeding him the pebble-sized snacks. "Wait until you see your other surprise."

As he was busy nibbling on his treats, Lilly started opening the box. Gently holding it in her hand, she lifted off the top. She soon put on a smile as she looked at the items.

"Are you ready for your next surprise?"

Finished with his last pebble treat, Mr. Prickles looked over at her and nodded his head.

"Close your eyes," she instructed him.

Being such a well-trained and mannered critter, he did as she instructed and closed his eyes.

Lilly then pulled out the surprise gifts from behind her back.

"Okay, you can open them now."

Mr. Prickles opened his eyes and looked at what she held in her hands. Being curious, he moved himself closer. In her right hand was a little red and white striped scarf. In her left hand was a similarly colored Christmas hat. He curiously sniffed both of them.

"It's your new winter outfit!" she excitedly explained. "With Christmas almost here and it getting colder, I asked mom if we could buy you something special to keep you warm. Isn't it cute?"

Mr. Prickles looked over his new outfit for a few more seconds, then finally nodded his head with approval.

"Come on! Let's see how it looks on you!"

Lilly took the scarf first and gently tied it around his chubby neck. Finally, she grabbed the soft hand-woven hat and placed it on his head.

"It's perfect! You look even more adorable than before. I didn't think that was even possible."

Mr. Prickles smiled at her compliment.

"Hold on, I'm going to get mom's phone, so I can take a picture of you. Wait right here."

Before leaving for the phone, Lilly grabbed the small mirror from atop her dresser and set it on the floor in front of him.

"Here, so you can see for yourself just how good you look," she said. "I'll be back in a minute."

As she headed downstairs, Mr. Prickles couldn't help but smile at his reflection. His new winter apparel filled him with a newfound sense of confidence.

Footsteps once again sounded through the hallway as Lilly returned.

"Okay, I've got her phone. Hold still while I take your picture," she told him. "Now smile for the camera and say cheese."

Mr. Prickles happily smiled and let out a squeak.

Lilly clicked the button and saved the picture. She told him she would ask her mom to post it online so the whole world could see his handsome appearance.

Mr. Prickles once again gave off a big smile.

Chapter 3

The first official day of winter break came, and as one would guess, Lilly was happy as could be. What kid wouldn't be full of joy knowing that they had two full weeks off of school? Not only that, but Christmas was just a week away. With those two things in her life, was it any wonder why she was smiling so much? Even while eating dinner, her parents couldn't help but notice her radiating endless joy.

"My, someone sure seems to be in a happy mood today. It wouldn't be because today was the last day of school, would it?" asked mom.

"Or maybe it's because Christmas is only one week away," said dad. "Which would mean that a particularly good girl is going to be getting a bunch of presents from Santa soon."

Lilly again smiled.

"You know, I heard a rumor online that said Santa is getting hungrier on his delivery rides and is now asking families to leave out more cookies for him. Specifically, the double chocolate chunk ones. He apparently likes those a lot."

"Yes, I bet he does," said mom with a smirk. "I'll remember to buy extra when we go to the store."

As they continued eating their dinner, Lilly was busy planning in her head all the fun things she wanted to do over Christmas break. Things such as sledding, making snowmen, decorating gingerbread houses. But above all, she was most excited about having more time to spend with Mr. Prickles.

Having finished her dinner, Lilly politely excused herself from the table, saying that she was going up to her room. Before she could leave, though, her mom's phone suddenly started ringing. Lilly was asked to go into the living room and grab it. She did so and saw that it was her grandma who was calling. Lilly quickly handed the phone over to her mom. With the small task done, she headed up to her room.

Upon entering, Lilly immediately heard a rustling sound coming from the little hedgehog house. It became clear that someone had woken up from his slumber. Making his way outside, Mr. Prickles stretched his arms and breathed in his evening air.

"Rise and shine, sleepy head," she said, greeting him.

As usual, Mr. Prickles first went to eat some pebbles from his little dish. After all, breakfast was the most important meal of the day. Once he was done munching on his food, he helped himself to a drink of water before finally going over to Lilly.

Pulling out a notebook from her backpack, she began showing him the list she had made earlier.

"Look, I wrote down all the things we're going to do over winter break. There's so much fun stuff here. See? We're going to do arts and crafts, build snowmen, sledding, and more. Remember how much fun we had last year? Well, this year is going to be even better. And with the new hat and scarf we got you, you're going to be even warmer now too."

Mr. Prickles looked as excited as she did.

As Lilly continued to unveil her many plans to him, a knock suddenly sounded from her door.

"Hey, sweetie, can we come in for a minute?" her dad asked.

"Yeah, me and Mr. Prickles are just talking."

The door soon opened, and both of her parents walked in. They unfortunately didn't look as lively and cheerful as they did at dinner. Sitting themselves down on her bed, they started talking.

"Sweetie, me and your mom need to tell you something. It's about some unhappy news. You see—" mom stopped him before he could finish his sentence.

"Let me tell her," she said, turning her full attention to Lilly. "I just got done talking to your grandma…" there was a pause in her voice as if struggling to say the words. "She told me that your grandpa is in the hospital. Something bad happened, and he's really sick."

"What's wrong with him? Does he have a cold?" Lilly innocently asked.

Her mom shook her head, trying to keep the worried tears in her eyes.

"No, sweetie. He had a problem with his heart."

"What's wrong with his heart? Is grandpa going to be okay?"

"Yes, the doctor said that he's okay for now. Thank God. But since he's sick, it means that he's really weak and can't move around."

"Is the doctor going to give him medicine so he can feel better?"

Mom couldn't help but smile a little at her daughter's innocent question.

"Yes, sweetie. The doctor is giving him medicine to help him feel better. Unfortunately, the medicine can only do so much. So, we're going to have to change our plans for Christmas. Your dad is going to buy us plane tickets for a flight tomorrow, which means we're going to be spending our Christmas in Arizona this year."

Much to her parent's surprise, Lilly didn't seem that sad about leaving home for the holidays. In fact, she seemed kind of excited.

"Did you hear that, Mr. Prickles? We're going to Grandma and Grandpa's for Christmas this year! You're going to be going on your first trip ever!" she excitedly said, holding him up to her face.

Her parents immediately looked at each other. It was obvious that they had forgotten to put the family hedgehog into consideration. Both of them soon met Lilly with a face of remorse.

"Sweetie, I think Mr. Prickles might have to stay with the neighbors while we're gone," dad explained. "We're going on the plane, which could be scary for him. He might not be able to handle something like that. Plus, it would cost us extra, and the tickets we're buying are going to be expensive enough as it is."

Lilly's face instantly sunk down as hearing those words left her feeling heartbroken.

"But we can't celebrate Christmas without Mr. Prickles. He's part of our family."

It was clear to her parents how devastated she was by the idea.

"Sweetie, I know that you always want to have Mr. Prickles beside you, but please try to understand, it might not be the best thing if we take him with us," dad again tried to explain, hoping to reason with her.

A tear finally began to fall from Lilly's eye.

"…but it won't be Christmas without him."

Both mom and dad again looked at each other. It became clear that they needed to figure something out.

Kneeling down beside her crying daughter, mom gently wiped the tear from her check.

"Don't cry, sweetie. We don't need two girls crying in this house," she softly told her. "Listen, we'll try to figure something out, okay? Don't be sad. I'm sure Mr. Prickles doesn't enjoy seeing you like this. Especially not after he got his new winter outfit."

Her words helped to lighten Lilly's spirit a little.

Seeing that their daughter was now more relaxed, and with everything explained, both mom and dad decided to leave her be and walked out the room, shutting the door. Once out in the privacy of the hallway, they looked at each other again, not knowing what to do.

"Well?" dad asked.

"Well, what?" replied mom.

"What are we going to do?"

"What can we do? You saw her. We have no choice but to take her hedgehog with us."

"Seriously?"

"Yep."

"No, seriously? Like for real?"

"Yes," she said for the last time.

"Alright. Looks like our family is taking a hedgehog on a plane. This should be interesting," he said. "I mean, I've heard of snakes on a plane, but never hedgehogs."

Mom tried to stop herself, but she couldn't help but giggle at his terrible joke. The smile on her face let him know she was doing her best to cope with the difficult situation.

"Thanks for trying to make this better," she told him.

Putting his hand over her shoulder and kissing her cheek, he said, "Hey, that's my job."

Chapter 4

Lilly and her parents had been waiting in the check-in line at the airport for nearly an hour. With it being the holidays, it was unsurprisingly extra busy. Hundreds of people just like them were eager to get on a plane and leave. Dozens of conversations were going on everywhere against the backdrop of Christmas music. With the worsening snowstorm, many were starting to wonder if they would even make their flights at all. Word even went around that some would be delayed.

Finally, as a few more minutes went by, they found themselves next in line to check-in to their flight. Lilly's dad went up to the lady attendant at the counter and handed her their tickets. She asked him some standard questions and went over the flight information. However, something soon seemed off as they talked.

"Wait, there has to be some mistake. That can't be right," he told the attendant.

"I'm sorry, sir, but we unfortunately can't allow the hedgehog as a carry-on. It'll have to go in the cargo area with the luggage."

"You've got to be kidding me!" he yelled. "On the website, it said that if the animal is small enough, that it can go under our seat. I even called to be sure, and they said that it was right. I mean, look at him. You can't get any smaller than a hedgehog," he said, pointing at Mr. Prickles, who was curiously looking outside through his little kennel.

"Yes, that's correct, but hedgehogs are unfortunately listed as exotic animals, which means they can't be inside the cabin. If it were anything else like a chihuahua or small cat, it'd be fine," she explained. "You should've been more specific when you spoke with the service representative."

It became clear by his face that he was extremely unhappy.

"I'm really sorry, sir, but it's the airline's rules," she said with honest empathy.

Lilly overheard some of the commotion and had a worried look on her face.

"Dad, what's going on? Mr. Prickles is still coming with us, right?"

"Yes, he's still coming with us," he reassured her. "It's just a little problem that I'm trying to fix."

Turning his attention back to the attendant, he tried his best to ask if she could somehow make an exception. Unfortunately, the answer was still no.

"I'm sorry, sir, but I would get in a lot of trouble if they found out that I let you take a hedgehog inside the cabin."

After saying that, however, the woman's attention finally turned to Lilly. She could see the worried look on her face as she clutched onto the kennel containing her prickly friend.

In a surprise gesture of kindness, the woman attendant left her post and walked over to them.

"Hello there," she greeted Lilly. "Is this your hedgehog?"

"Yes," she timidly answered.

"I've never seen a hedgehog wearing a hat and scarf before. It looks really cute. What's its name?"

"His name is Mr. Prickles. That's his winter outfit."

"I see," she said, eying him through the kennel. "Well, as I was telling your father here, the airline unfortunately has a rule that says he'll have to go inside underneath the plane."

The words put an intense look of concern on Lilly's face. It looked like she was about to cry.

"Don't worry though," the woman continued. "I can guarantee you that Mr. Prickles will be safe and that no harm will come to him. He may get a little scared, as most animals do, but it's only temporary. When you guys land, you'll have him right back in your arms just like you do right now."

Seeing how stressed she looked, Lilly's mom finally knelt down beside her.

"Sweetie, I know you don't want to be separated from Mr. Prickles, but it's the only option we have," she explained to

Lilly, who held tightly onto the kennel. "The nice woman here said that he'll be taken good care of. Please understand, he isn't going anywhere. He'll be right under where we're sitting. He's going to be safe. Do you understand, sweetie?"

Lilly nodded her head yes.

"Okay, now please kindly hand over Mr. Prickles to the nice lady."

Lilly nodded her head again. Before handing him over, though, she looked at him one last time through the kennel.

"You're going to be by yourself for a little while, Mr. Prickles. The mean people who work on the plane said that you can't sit with us. I know. They're being big bullies just like some of the kids at school."

Mr. Prickles solemnly sunk his head and let out a sad sigh. He understood exactly what was happening just by the timbre in her voice.

"You're going to be safe though. The lady here said that they're going to take care of you," she explained. "Promise me that you won't get scared, okay? Just think of it like being on your own little adventure."

Mr. Prickles nodded his head, giving her a reassuring smile.

With that said, Lilly told her hedgehog one last time that she loved him. Finally, she handed the kennel over to the lady.

Taking the kennel to the scale on the counter, she recorded the weight and then tagged it with the name 'Mr. Prickles' typed in bold font. She even added a note reading 'very special cargo' next to it. With that done, she placed him on a cart to be taken with the luggage to the plane. Lilly then waved bye to her best friend as they finally took him away.

"Come on, sweetie. Let's go find our terminal. After that, we'll go to one of the vending machines and buy you some candy."

The promise of a sweet treat from her mom helped to put a small smile on Lilly's face.

* * *

Outside on the tarmac where all the planes parked, a group of workers was busy loading the passenger luggage inside the underbelly compartment of the plane.

"How much more do we have left?" asked one of the men. "It's freezing out here. I want to get inside before I turn into a snowman."

"This next truck coming up is the last of it," said the boss. "Then we can go on break."

"I thought we still had to do a load for the international delivery flight?" asked one of the other workers.

"Yeah, but we don't have to start on that for another hour."

"Okay, that's good to hear. I'm going to get me a nice hot cup of coffee as soon as we finish this then."

Soon after, the last truck arrived.

The workers all began grabbing the bags and suitcases, loading them into the plane. Right at the very end on the bed of the truck was Mr. Prickles. He remained safely inside his kennel with his hat and scarf keeping him warm. Unfortunately, it would be a few more minutes before they reached him.

Piece by piece, they loaded the plane. However, something unexpected soon happened. Another truck arrived and parked right next to the one they were working on. This one was different though. Instead of passenger luggage, it carried dozens of different-sized cardboard boxes with labels on them.

"Hey, guys! I've just got word that the next plane got pushed forward on its departure time," the driver announced.

All of the workers moaned and groaned simultaneously at the unwelcome news.

"What?! Why?!" the boss asked.

"Because of the blizzard on the way," he answered. "They're expecting all flights within the next hour to get delayed, and they can't afford to keep it grounded."

Almost immediately, all of the workers started speeding up their efforts to get everything loaded onto the passenger plane. They passed each other luggage faster than they could store it. Unfortunately, with them moving so fast, they naturally got sloppy. Unsurprisingly, right next to the plane, a tower of luggage began forming. No one seemed to notice just how tall it was getting, as they were all going crazy trying to stuff up the compartments in a speedy manner.

After another minute of the frenzy, they were finally down to the last two items. One of them being the small kennel that held Mr. Prickles. The youngest of the workers was the one who noticed him there.

"Hey, I've got a pet here! It looks like a hedgehog!" he yelled over to his boss.

"Just go and put it with the other animals," he instructed him.

He gently picked up the kennel and was ready to take him to be put inside. However, something stopped him from moving forward. Looking over at the luggage tower, the young worker saw that it was starting to wobble.

"Look out! It's going to fall over!" he warned everyone.

Setting Mr. Prickles down onto the bed of the truck, the young man ran over to try and stop it from falling. Unfortunately, he was too late. Within a second, all the bags of luggage and suitcases came crashing down. It was a giant mess. Fortunately, no one was hurt. The boss was really mad though. He was so furious that his face started turning red, even in the cold weather.

"Great! Just great!" he yelled. "Look at this mess! It's going to take us another five minutes to clean up!"

Realizing that they didn't have any more time to waste, he decided to split up his crew.

"Okay, you two, stay here and finish loading this plane. You two, come with me to start on the next one."

The workers all nodded their heads and followed his orders. Two of them stayed behind to finish the passenger plane, while the rest got on the truck carrying the boxes and left.

After a few more minutes, the passenger plane was finally loaded. They were about to close the door, but the same young worker from before suddenly remembered the hedgehog and ran over to grab it. When he arrived, however, he discovered something. The kennel was missing.

"What happened to that hedgehog?" he asked with confusion. "It should be here. When I saw all that luggage falling, I set him down right—" he stopped himself, suddenly realizing what must've happened.

With the trucks having been parked so close to one another, he must have put it on the one with all the boxes by accident.

"Uh oh."

The young worker urgently tried to tell someone, but it was too late. The plane carrying Lilly and her family had started its engines. Soon, it was being signaled for departure by the people on the runway. All he could do was watch from afar as it got ready for takeoff. Within a minute, the plane rolled forward and eventually flew into the air.

Back on the ground at the other end of the airport was a lonely hedgehog being loaded onto a cargo plane by a worker who didn't even notice him. It was obvious to Mr. Prickles that something was wrong, but he couldn't do anything about it. Pretty soon, everything around him got dark as he was buried by dozens of boxes destined to go to unknown places. Finally, the cargo door closed, and the engines roared as the plane got ready to leave. All Mr. Prickles could do was shake in his little kennel. Not because he was cold, but because he was scared. What hedgehog wouldn't have been? Lilly was right when she said it would be like going on an adventure; he just didn't know how right.

And finally, just like that, a lone hedgehog wearing a hat and scarf went up, soaring into the clouds.

Chapter 5

From outside the window, everything on the ground seemed so tiny. At 20,000 feet in the air, Lilly couldn't help but look in awe at the scenic view. To her, all the cities, towns, and sections of farmland resembled a giant knitted quilt. For a second, she thought about picking up Mr. Prickles and showing him the view, but she soon remembered that she couldn't. Eventually, the plane found its way into a giant cloud, obscuring everything from sight. Soon after, the lady flight attendant came by and offered them some snacks.

"Hello, would you folks like something to eat or drink?" she asked.

"Just a water for me and my wife," Lilly's dad told her.

"And for the little one?"

"Can I have hot chocolate?" asked Lilly.

"Of course you can," she gladly replied. "Do you want it with marshmallows or without?"

"With marshmallows, please."

"Coming right up," she told her, grabbing the pitcher from the cart and pouring the warm drink. "Here you go."

"Thank you."

"You're very welcome," she said. "We also have some holiday cookies if you're interested."

Lilly immediately smiled and nodded her head.

"You have a choice between gingerbread men and Christmas tree cookies."

"I want the gingerbread men."

The nice attendant reached down into the bottom of her cart and pulled out a small pouch of cookies. Lilly thanked her once again, allowing her to move on to the next passengers.

"Geez, you sure are eating a lot of sweets today," dad commented. "You better be sure to brush your teeth double good when we get to your grandma's house."

"It's okay," said mom. "She's had a rough morning. Some sugar and chocolate will do her good."

While enjoying her delicious treats, Lilly turned her attention back to the window. The clouds had all disappeared, allowing her to see the wide expansion below again. After a while, she noticed the green plains gradually turning into desert. Even though she knew it was still mid-December, seeing the bright sun made her think for a moment that it was summer. If it wasn't for the gingerbread cookie in her hand, she would've thought that it really was. But as she had learned in school, states in the southwestern part of the United States stayed warm throughout the entire year. She realized it would not be the normal Christmas she was used to. With no snow around, it would surely be a big change.

After another hour of flying, the plane finally landed at the airport. Lilly and her parents grabbed their carry-on bags and walked out to the arrival terminal. Making their way to the baggage claim area, they patiently waited amongst the crowd to grab their belongings. One by one, dozens of suitcases and animal kennels swerved around the baggage carousel. Lilly was eager to see Mr. Prickles show up. While she waited, she saw a bunch of cats and dogs being picked up by their owners. She even saw a lady pick up her pet iguana.

Several minutes went by, however, and they soon realized that they were the only people left. Eagerly watching the conveyor belt, they noticed that it had stopped moving. They had all of their other belongings except for one very important thing—the kennel holding their pet hedgehog. It was finally to the point where Lilly was getting worried.

"Dad, where's Mr. Prickles?" she asked, appearing worried.

"I don't know, sweetie," he answered with honesty. "Listen, you and mom stay here and keep watch. I'm going to go and ask the man at the desk to see if he can find out anything."

They did as they were told and patiently waited, hoping that their beloved pet would show up.

After several minutes of talking to the service employee and his manager, Lilly's dad was finally given the unpleasant news. They informed him that their pet was never loaded onto the plane. That there was an accidental mix-up with the cargo. He asked if there was a way to get him flown back to them. The manager regretfully told him that the plane he most likely ended up on was an international delivery flight, and that getting a hold of them would be very difficult, as it was right in the middle of the busy holiday season. He pleaded with the manager to try and find some way to get their pet back, making it known that it belonged to his daughter. Feeling awful about the situation, the sympathetic man gave him the name and number of a higher-up to call, saying they were sorry and that they unfortunately couldn't do more. Feeling defeated and helpless, he realized he had no choice but to tell Lilly what had happened. He didn't want to, but he knew he had to.

"Did you find out where Mr. Prickles is?" asked Lilly as he returned.

"Sweetie...I'm afraid I have some bad news."

He explained to her everything that had happened. Mom was shocked by the news. Before either parent could do anything, an unbearable frown formed on Lilly's face, followed by a waterfall of tears. The sound of a young girl crying was then heard throughout the airport. They were the cries of a broken heart. Both mom and dad kneeled down to hug and comfort her, but no matter how hard they hugged, the tears just wouldn't stop. For poor Lilly, Christmas was ruined.

Chapter 6

After several hours of flying miles across the sky, the delivery plane eventually made its landing down on the runway. Just exactly where it landed, however, remained a mystery. The engine soon shut off, and the pilots exited. A group of workers then arrived and opened the large cargo door, preparing themselves to unload all the pallets containing boxes. One by one, they started taking out and loading the boxes onto delivery trucks. While unloading one of the pallets, however, a young worker noticed an unexpected item.

"Qu'est-ce que c'est?" he asked in a thick French accent.

Upon closer inspection, he discovered that the item in question was a small kennel holding a hedgehog wearing a hat and scarf. Picking it up, he curiously looked inside at the little critter.

"C'est un hérisson."

Thinking it peculiar that a hedgehog was among the hundreds of packages, the young worker decided to call his boss over to check it out.

"Patron! Pouvez-vous inspecter?"

An older man with a thin mustache soon approached.

Oui?"

"J'ai trouvé ça."

"Un hérisson?" he said, looking at the frightened hedgehog.

"Oui."

The boss grabbed the kennel and checked to see if it had a label or any written information as to where it came from. Finally, he noticed the tag.

"Monsieur Prickles," he read aloud from it. "Importante cargaison."

It quickly became obvious to him that it came from the United States.

"C'est un hérisson américain," he informed the young worker.

Both of them then noticed that the little hedgehog seemed scared and was shaking. The boss asked the worker if he knew any English, hoping that hearing familiar words would help calm it down. He nodded his head and said that he'd been studying English for a few months at university. Seeing that it was the only option they had to prevent the critter from having a panic attack, he handed him back the kennel so that he could try to calm it down.

"Um…Bonjour, Mr. Prickles," he greeted him with a friendly smile. "My name is Stefan. Um…welcome to Paris."

Even though he was trying his best to appear as friendly as possible, it was clear to Stefan that he was still a very startled hedgehog. Then, thinking quickly, he remembered the bag of sunflower seeds in his pocket that he had been saving. Pulling it out and opening it up, he offered him some to eat.

Almost immediately, Mr. Prickles stopped shaking and cautiously went to sniff the food in Stefan's fingers. He was a little hesitant at first to take food from a stranger, but Mr. Prickles soon gave in and started munching on it.

Seeing that the hedgehog had calmed down, the boss told Stefan to go inside the terminal and drop it off at customs so that he could report it.

While walking on the tarmac, Mr. Prickles peeked out of his kennel and caught sight of the Eiffel tower in the far distance. It became abundantly clear to him that he was far away from home. While anxious about being separated from his family, he still couldn't help but look in awe at the beautiful view. The Parisian skyline was unlike anything he had ever seen before.

Making their way inside the airport, Stefan suddenly noticed a girl who he liked a lot working over at the café stand. She surprisingly went to the same university as he did and was even in the same English class as him too. Wanting to brighten up her day a little, he decided to show her the hedgehog he had discovered.

"Hey, Charlotte."

"Hey, Stefan. What are you doing here?" she asked. "I thought you were busy unloading the planes."

"I was, but they sent me inside to report some very important cargo to customs."

"Really, what?"

He lifted the small kennel to the counter and showed her.

"Here, check it out."

She curiously looked inside and was immediately spellbound.

"Aww!" she said, her eyes lighting up instantly.

"Yeah, we found him buried behind a bunch of packages."

"Does he have a name?"

"It says here his name is Mr. Prickles," he replied, pointing his finger to the tag.

"Look at his little hat and scarf! He's so adorable!"

"Yeah, he's a cute little guy."

"Can I hold him?" she asked.

"Um…I'm not sure if I'm allowed to—"

"Please, I really want to hold him and take a picture with him. I promise I'll be careful."

Not wanting to disappoint the girl he had a crush on and deny her a chance of happiness, he agreed.

"Alright," he said, opening the gate.

Charlotte called Mr. Prickles' name while letting out a friendly chirping noise.

"Come outside, Mr. Prickles. Come on. I bet you've been in there for a long time and want to move your feet around."

Mr. Prickles immediately got scared and retreated to the opposite end of his kennel. Charlotte frowned at his reaction.

"Here, try this," said Stefan, handing her the bag of seeds.

She grabbed a couple of pieces and offered them to him. It took a few seconds, but Mr. Prickles eventually went up to her hand and grabbed the bits of food. While busy munching away, Charlotte saw her chance and gently picked him up. Much to their surprise, he didn't get startled when she held him. Softly gliding her fingers across his quills, she started petting him. Once he was done eating his snack, Mr. Prickles decided to walk around on the counter. Carefully watching him, she let him move around at his leisure to stretch his feet. However, she that noticed that it looked like he was trying to look for something. He just kept bobbing his nose around, eagerly searching the area.

"He must be thirsty," said Stefan.

"Yeah, I think you're right," agreed Charlotte. "Here, watch him; I'm going to get some water."

She grabbed a pitcher from the fridge and poured some cool water into a little bowl.

"Here you go," she said, placing the bowl in front of him. "Drink up, little guy."

As Mr. Prickles drank his water, Charlotte handed Stefan her phone.

"Here, take a picture of me with him."

Charlotte then kneeled down beside the counter and leveled herself with Mr. Prickles.

"Smile and say cheese!"

Being such a well-trained and mannered hedgehog, Mr. Prickles lifted his head and smiled at the camera. Seeing the critter smile on command took Stefan by surprise. Not wanting to miss the moment, he clicked the capture button.

"Got it!"

"Great, let me see," she said, taking her phone back. "Oh my God! We look so cute! Here, I'm going to post it online, so everyone can see that we're friends." Within a few seconds, the image was shared for the whole world to see.

"Okay, well, I really have to take him to customs now," Stefan informed her.

Charlotte looked sad for a moment, but she knew that Mr. Prickles couldn't stay with her forever. That he probably had a family waiting for him to return. Gently picking him up again, she placed him back in the kennel.

"Looks like it's time for you to go. I'm really glad that I got the chance to meet you, Mr. Prickles. Don't ever forget me. I promise I'll never forget about you."

As they walked away, Charlotte waved bye one last time while wishing Mr. Prickles a merry Christmas. She also thanked Stefan for bringing him over to her.

As instructed by his boss, Stefan reported him to customs. He explained what had happened and where they found him. They told him they would look up the information on the tag and have it returned to his owners. Realizing that it was probably the last time he would see Mr. Prickles, Stefan said a heartfelt goodbye and gave him some more sunflower seeds for his trip. Then, he finally waved bye and left.

After some time of waiting in customs, a worker eventually came by, picked him up, and took him to the next flight leaving for the United States. Everything seemed to be settled for the lost hedgehog. Unfortunately, the unthinkable happened on the way. Believe it or not, the same thing that happened on the tarmac back home happened to him again. Through sheer accident and bad luck, Mr. Prickles was put on the wrong truck and taken to another delivery plane. And just like that, he was up in the air again. To what destination remained a mystery.

Chapter 7

"You need to eat something, dear. A young girl like you shouldn't go so long without having some food in their stomach," said grandma.

"I'm not hungry," Lilly replied, keeping her head sunk down on the dinner table.

It was clear to grandma and mom that she was still very emotional over what happened.

"Sweetie, please don't be like this. I know you're sad that Mr. Prickles got lost, but your dad said that he's going to keep calling the airline to see if they can find him," said mom.

"But what if they can't find him? What if I never see him again?" asked Lilly, still in tears. "I need him, and he needs me. I can't stop thinking about how scared he must be right now."

"Don't think like that, sweetie. Don't give up hope. I know you're scared and worried about him, but you shouldn't be filling your head with such negative thoughts."

Her words unfortunately didn't stop the tears from falling.

"Your mother's right, dear," said grandma, sitting herself down next to her. "I know it's hard to be hopeful in trying times like this, but you have to keep your head up," she said, putting her hand over Lilly's. "You know, when your grandpa got sick a couple nights ago, I was really scared, just like you are right now. I didn't know what was going to happen. I honestly thought I was going to lose him forever. But even though I was scared, I told myself not to give up hope…would you like to know what I did that kept me hopeful?"

"Yes, tell me."

"I thought about all the great memories your grandpa and I shared together. As I did that, I said a prayer. I prayed for him to get better. Soon after I did that, the doctor came up to me and said that your grandpa's heart was doing better. You see, dear, you can't ever give up hope; even in the darkest of times," offering her other hand to Lilly, she asked: "Do you want to say a prayer for Mr. Prickles together?"

Lilly nodded her head and said yes.

From the corner, Lilly's mom wiped the tear off her eye as she watched them pray together. Hearing her mother's words about her father reminded her of how grateful she felt he was still with them. Deciding to leave them alone to their prayer, she headed up the stairs to the bedroom to spend some more time with her recovering father.

Meanwhile, in the living room, Lilly's dad was once again busy talking on the phone.

"Yes, I understand that he got put on the wrong plane. That's already been established for the hundredth time. What I want to know is where he was taken to," he told the airline representative.

They put him on hold for a few minutes, saying that they were going to check again for any reports of a found hedgehog. All he could do was patiently wait. Finally, after several minutes, the representative returned with great news.

"They did?! Where?!" dad asked with excitement.

The representative explained the information to him.

"In Europe?! Where in Europe?!"

The representative once again made him patiently wait so he could find out the exact location. After a couple more minutes, they returned and gave him the information.

"In Paris!!" he shouted with disbelief.

The representative went on to further explain all of the information they had so far gathered.

"Yes, yes, please. Thank you very much. You have no idea how much of a relief this is for us," he appreciatively thanked them before finally hanging up the phone. He couldn't wait to tell his family the great news.

Back in the bedroom, Lilly's mom was busy covering up her still feeble father with a blanket. His body still hadn't fully recovered and was in need of more rest and sleep. Wanting to get her mind off things for a little bit, she decided to go on her phone and look at the many pictures people had posted online. She scrolled through the trending section. There were pictures of families celebrating Christmas together, people on vacations, festive parties, and literally everything else that a person could think of. While scrolling through all of them, she soon came across one particular image that was getting thousands of likes. It was a picture of a girl and a hedgehog that looked suspiciously like Mr. Prickles. It even had the same winter outfit and everything. She then noticed that it was from Paris, though, and told herself that there was no way, seeing it as just a coincidence. However, she soon noticed the caption that read: *Me and Mr. Prickles, a cute hedgehog from the United States.* Mom's eyes instantly opened wide, and she almost dropped her phone. She couldn't believe it. She had discovered where Mr. Prickles was.

Wanting to announce the news to everyone, she quickly ran out into the hallway, making her way down to the kitchen where Lilly was at. At the same time, the other parent was making his way to the kitchen as well. Finally, without warning, they both crashed into each other.

"Oh!—I'm so sorry. I didn't see you. Are you okay?" dad asked.

"Yeah, I'm fine," she said. "But I have great news!"

"Me too!"

They quickly told each other what they had discovered. Neither of them could believe it. Soon, they made their way into the kitchen together to tell their daughter.

"Lilly!" both simultaneously spoke. "We found out where Mr. Prickles is at!"

Chapter 8

After a couple hours of flying, the delivery plane lowered its landing gear and touched down on the airport runway. As before, Mr. Prickles was buried deep behind a stack of boxes. The doors soon opened and a group of workers entered inside to unload everything.

"Beeil dich und entlade das Flugzeud!" shouted a woman wearing a supervisor's uniform. "Der Schneestrurm naht!" It was clear by her voice that she was ordering the workers to hurry up unloading the plane, as a snowstorm was reported to be on the way. Hands and feet were moving so fast that no one seemed to notice that a kennel with a hedgehog was among the boxes.

"Alles fertig!" said one of the workers, announcing that the plane was finally emptied out.

"Gut," she replied. "Dann lass uns reingehen."

She and her crew of workers then got onto the cargo truck and headed back inside the airport.

Peering out through his kennel, Mr. Prickles was more than a little confused by his outside surroundings. As before, he knew he was somewhere very far away from home. Looking in the distance, he saw a sign that read: Berlin Brandenburg Airport.

A flurry of snow started falling as soon as they got inside. It didn't take long for it to cover everything under a cold white blanket. A voice on the loudspeaker then announced to everyone in the airport that all flights were being delayed until morning due to the weather, leaving hundreds stranded. Unfortunately, there was nothing anyone could do. The snow was just too much.

Minutes turned into hours for many, including Mr. Prickles, who idly waited inside his kennel, hoping to be discovered. However, the storage area in which they put him inside was unfortunately very large in size. It resembled a large warehouse. To make matters worse, the workers ended up putting him high atop a mountain of boxes. It also didn't help that they turned all the lights off, engulfing him in darkness.

For any other animal, it would've been a nightmare, but Mr. Prickles was used to the dark, with him having been a nocturnal creature and all. Although, leaving one light on would've still been a nice gesture since he liked nightlights. A bigger concern to him was how long it would take to be reunited with Lilly. It had been a real challenge for him, having been separated for so long. After all, nearly two days had passed since they were last together. It wasn't just Lilly he missed either; he missed his entire family. The family that treated him so well and showered him with so many gifts. He could only imagine that they missed him just as much. Feeling sad, he started rubbing his paw on his scarf to remind himself of their love. Feeling the warmth of it was enough to give him some much-needed hope. After realizing that it would be awhile before anyone showed up, he finally decided to take a nap and catch some Z's.

More than two hours of silence had passed. Then, without warning, all the lights turned on, and a door opened. Mr. Prickles woke up almost instantly. Two people soon entered the storage area. One of them was the woman from earlier who was in charge of unloading the plane. The other was a man wearing a pilot's uniform.

"Sorry, I wish I spoke more German, but my vocabulary is still severely limited. The only words I know are 'ja', 'nein', and 'guten tag," said the pilot.

"Well, that's better than nothing. Luckily for you, English is my second language."

"I'm glad. It sure saves me a lot of trouble," he said. "So, where's the cargo manifest for the flight? I was told to double-check on some of the items since the flight got delayed."

"It's over here—follow me. Oh, and you can call me Johanna."

Watching from afar, Mr. Prickles realized his chance at getting discovered had come. He had no idea how long he would possibly end up staying there, and he didn't intend on finding out. Thinking quickly, he started doing the only thing he could do to get their attention.

While Johanna was busy going through the documents in the office, the pilot soon overheard a peculiar sound coming from somewhere behind them.

"Do you hear that?" he asked.

"No, I don't hear anything."

"Well, I do. It sounds like a squeak."

"A squeak?"

"Yes, a squeak," he repeated. "Shh…listen…do you hear it?"

"Yes, I do now," she confirmed. "Maybe it's a mouse. This is a pretty big building—there's bound to be some mice around."

"No, it's not a mouse," he said. "It's something else."

They both finally decided to go and investigate, searching throughout the area, trying to find the source of the mysterious squeak. Eventually, the pilot discovered it.

"Hey, look up there," he said, pointing to the kennel sitting high atop the boxes. "Is that an animal kennel?"

"Yes, I think it is," said Johanna with bewilderment. "How'd it get up there?"

"I don't know, but it certainly doesn't belong up there, that's for sure."

The pilot started carefully climbing up the mountain of boxes. It ended up being higher than it looked.

"Got it!" he said, grabbing onto the kennel.

"What is it?"

Making his way back down, he happily showed her.

"It's a hedgehog."

"A hedgehog?! How'd a hedgehog get all the way in here?" she asked.

"Beats me, but here it is."

Johanna smiled at Mr. Prickles. "It's adorable! Look, it's wearing a little hat and scarf!"

The pilot agreed. "Yes, you don't see that every day."

Finally, she noticed the tag on the side.

"It says here his name is Mr. Prickles and that he's from the United States."

"He must've gotten lost and somehow ended up here," the pilot guessed. "We should probably report him to customs."

"How?" asked Johanna. "They closed everything down because of the storm, remember?"

"Oh yeah, that's right."

"What should we do with him?"

The pilot kept on looking at Mr. Prickles with keen curiosity. Something about the critter just captivated his attention.

Johanna remained unsure of what to do. She couldn't report Mr. Prickles to anyone, and she also didn't want to leave him there, as she wasn't sure how long it had been since he ate anything. The pilot seemed a little worried about him as well. The clock was unfortunately ticking though, as they both had to leave in a matter of minutes. A decision needed to be made quickly.

"Wait. I think I have an idea," Johanna finally said.

"What?"

"Well, we actually have a hedgehog at my house. It belongs to my six-year-old son," she explained. "It's the only pet that we could get since he's allergic to most others. I…I could take him home for the night and report him to customs tomorrow."

"That sounds like a good idea. But, unfortunately, I think it might be against the rules," the pilot informed her.

"I know it is, but I can't just leave him here. Who knows how long the storm will last? Plus, he's probably hungry, and we have food to feed him at my house."

The pilot seemed reluctant to allow her to take Mr. Prickles at first, but after much deliberation, he gave his okay.

"Fine, I guess we can keep this as our little secret. Just be sure you report him to customs as soon as the weather clears."

"I will. Thank you."

They soon returned to the office, where Johanna handed him the cargo manifest that he was looking for. After that, they turned out the lights and walked out with Mr. Prickles in hand.

"By the way, do you know what the German word for hedgehog is?" she asked the pilot.

"No, what is it?"

"It's Igel."

"Igel…hmm, I didn't know that. Guess that's another word I can add to my vocabulary now."

* * *

Peering out of the car window, Mr. Prickles gazed in awe at the Berlin cityscape in front of him. He immediately noticed how different everything was compared to back home. From the roads to the houses, it was a big cultural change for sure. Everything looked so beautiful too, especially with all the Christmas decorations and festive lights illuminating every building and street block. The people appeared so much happier as well. Everyone was just so cheery. Maybe because it was Christmas, or maybe it was simply the German way of life.

Johanna eventually drove out of the city and into the neighboring suburbs. The homes were similar to the ones back where Mr. Prickles lived. So much so that they reminded him of his home. Finally, after one more street turn, they arrived at Johanna's house.

"I'm home!" she announced, walking inside with the kennel in hand.

Almost immediately, her young son came running from the kitchen to greet her with a welcoming hug. Her husband naturally followed behind.

"Mama!"

"Hallo, Gunther!"

After a few seconds, her husband finally took notice of the kennel.

"Was ist da drin?" he asked, curious as to what she brought home.

"It's a surprise from work. I'll explain everything; you just have to promise to speak English when I take him out. I think hearing English makes him feel more comfortable. That goes for you too, Gunther. I know you're still learning, but just try your best."

Gunther and his father nodded their heads, agreeing to her request.

With that, she set the kennel down onto the floor and opened it, revealing their hedgehog guest.

"His name is Mr. Prickles. We found him in the package shipping area. He somehow ended up here all the way from the United States."

Gunther went down to the floor and greeted him with a friendly smile.

"Hi, Mr. Prickles," he said, readjusting his glasses. "My name is Gunther."

Mr. Prickles cautiously walked out towards him and sniffed around his face, eventually rubbing onto his nose.

"Hehe, hey, that tickles!"

Mr. Prickles let out a playful squeak in response.

"Wow! I can't believe you came here all the way from America! They must really take care of hedgehogs over there. They even gave you clothes to wear."

Gunther was awed by Mr. Prickles. He'd never seen another hedgehog like him before, and he had seen a lot of hedgehogs.

"How long do we get to keep him?" he curiously asked.

"Just for tonight, I'm afraid. I have to report him to customs tomorrow and hopefully get him sent back to his family. I bet they're really worried about him," Johanna explained.

"Is it okay if I take him upstairs to meet Holland?"

"Sure," she replied. "Just remember to be careful with him. Also, give him some food while you're introducing him to Holland."

"Okay, I will!" he said, grabbing Mr. Prickles with excitement and taking him up to his bedroom.

Gunther gave Mr. Prickles a quick tour of his room before finally setting him down on the bed. He told him to wait there while he turned around to the little blue igloo sitting in the corner next to his nightstand. Within a couple seconds, a white-quilled hedgehog appeared in his hands.

"Mr. Prickles, this is Holland. Holland, this is Mr. Prickles. Say hi."

It was the first time Mr. Prickles had seen another hedgehog since he was born. They both curiously eyed each other and soon started sniffing each other out. Holland, being a curious critter, noticed the hat and scarf and started sniffing them too. Mr. Prickles liked the attention he was getting. As a gesture of kindness, he patted Holland on his head. And just like that, a new friendship was made. Both hedgehogs had smiles on their faces.

As they were busy getting acquainted with one another, Gunther went to his drawer and grabbed some pellets for them to munch on.

Just like Lilly back home, Gunther also had a strong, deep love for hedgehogs. He considered Holland to be his best friend in the world. There were pictures of them together all over his dresser. Gunther even had a Sonic the Hedgehog poster on his wall too. It seemed as if hedgehog lovers were the same throughout much of the world.

"Here's some food for you guys. I brought some water too," he told them, placing the bowls down. "If you want more, just let me know."

Mr. Prickles dove right into the bowl because he was so hungry. It was the first full meal he'd eaten in nearly a day. The water was certainly refreshing too.

"Hey, when you're done eating, I'll show you all the toys that me and Holland usually play with. I know you're going to love them."

The promise of toys brought a smile to Mr. Prickles. He could hardly wait. Who knew Germany could be so much fun? Especially for a hedgehog.

Chapter 9

"Did they say when they're going to call or how long it's going to take for the plane to arrive from Paris?" asked Lilly's mom, who was sitting on the couch with her.

"No, they didn't give me any specifics," replied dad. "They just said that they're going to put him on the next flight to the U.S. and that the airport would call when it lands."

"I can't wait to see Mr. Prickles again," said Lilly. "I still can't believe he went all the way to Paris. Who would've thought? Not only that, but he made a new friend too."

"Yes, that Charlotte girl seemed really nice. The message reply she sent asking us to send her a picture of Mr. Prickles when he gets back was really sweet."

Lilly started showing a look of curiosity.

"Mom, I was wondering, what do they call hedgehogs in France anyway?"

"I don't know. Why don't we look it up?"

After a quick search for a translation, they found out what it was.

"It says here that the French word for hedgehog is 'hérisson.'"

"Hérisson?"

"Yep, sounds fancy, doesn't it?"

"Yeah, I like it. I'm going to start calling him that from now on."

As they were searching through other French words and talking amongst themselves, the phone unexpectedly started ringing again. Dad immediately picked it up and answered, hoping that it was good news from the airport.

"Hello?—Yes, this is he."

The voice on the other end soon began explaining the new situation concerning their lost hedgehog. Lilly and her mom both moved in closer, trying to listen in to the conversation, anxiously wondering if Mr. Prickles had made it back. Unfortunately, the somber change in dad's expression and voice made it clear that something was wrong.

"What do you mean he wasn't on board the flight? Didn't you have someone check him on the plane?" he asked, sounding upset.

Without hesitation, mom put her hand around Lilly's to comfort her, as they were suddenly expecting unpleasant news. The look of apprehension was over both of their faces.

"Well, do you at least know where he is?"

The voice on the other end said that they didn't and that no one had yet reported a hedgehog fitting the description.

"How could this have happened again?" he asked, sounding very unhappy. "This is unacceptable. I don't see how it's possible that he could've gotten lost twice."

The voice on the phone sounded remorseful, telling him they were very sorry for the unfortunate turn of events, and that they would call him as soon as they found out any new information.

Knowing there was nothing more he could do, Lilly's dad simply ended the conversation, hanging up the phone. The look of regret was all over his face, as he had the burden of telling his family the bad news.

"That was a representative from the airline. They said that Mr. Prickles somehow got lost again. They don't know how it happened. All they said was that they're doing everything they can to find out where he went. I'm really sorry. I know it isn't the news that you guys wanted to hear."

Lilly could see the look of guilt and sorrow in her father's eyes. She was saddened by the news, but she also understood how much effort he had been putting into getting her beloved hedgehog back and that he probably felt as if he had let her down.

"It's okay, dad. It's not your fault. I know you care about him a lot too. It's like grandma said though, we can't give up hope yet."

Hearing those words brought out newfound smiles from both her parents. Seeing their daughter handling such a difficult situation like that inspired them to remain hopeful and resilient as well.

"Did someone mention my name?" grandma asked as she walked into the living room, carrying a tray of cookies and hot chocolate.

"Oh, it was just Lilly, giving us some of your eternal wisdom," answered mom.

"Well, that's good to hear. I'm glad my granddaughter listened to what this old woman has to say."

"Yes, I'm glad too."

"Well, here. I thought I'd bring you some treats to munch on. Nothing says Christmas like a stomach full of fresh-baked cookies and hot chocolate."

"As always, you know just when to come in with the uplifting goodies," she said, helping Lilly and herself to some of the newly brought treats.

"That's what I'm here for."

"How's dad doing anyway? The last time I checked on him he was busy sleeping."

"He actually just woke up a couple minutes ago. I took him a cup of hot chocolate right before I came down here. He's doing much better now. I'm hoping that he'll be well enough by tomorrow to walk again. Go and talk to him. He's just up there watching tv."

"Yes, I think I will," she continued by asking Lilly's dad, "You want to come too?"

He agreed, and they both went upstairs to visit grandpa.

Silently sitting in the living room together, grandma couldn't help but notice the worried look on Lilly's face.

"Okay, spill it. Tell me what happened."

Lilly was silent at first, not wanting to impart the bad news to her.

"It's about Mr. Prickles, isn't it?"

She was hesitant at first, not wanting to say the bad news herself, but she knew that grandma would probably help to make her feel better.

"Yes, they said that he got lost again."

The news came as a shock to grandma.

"Dear, oh dear. That isn't good news at all."

Lilly began showing the inner sorrow and worry that she tried to hide from her parents earlier.

"I'm scared. I know you said that I shouldn't give up hope, but I'm scared that I'm never going to see him again."

Grandma took one more sip of her hot chocolate before setting it down on the table.

"Do you remember what we said when we prayed yesterday? We prayed for Mr. Prickles to return to us by Christmas. Well, last time I checked, the calendar said Christmas is still three days away. There's still time left. Remember Lilly, you can't give up hope. I know it's hard but keep your head up... Hey, listen, if you feel like you're losing the only hope you have left, well, then do what I do and search for new hope. There's always new hope somewhere in the world."

One of grandma's enduring words had caught Lilly's attention.

"Search," she whispered to herself. "Wait…I think I have an idea."

Seeing that her mom's phone was still on the table, she quickly picked it up and started browsing through the millions of pictures that people had posted online. Finally, she went on the search bar and typed in '#mrprickles'. Within a second, she found what she was hoping for.

"Oh my God! Oh my God!" she cheered. "I found him! Look! I've found Mr. Prickles!"

The screen showed a photograph of Mr. Prickles next to a boy with glasses and another hedgehog with white quills. The excitement in Lilly's voice resonated throughout the entire house. So much so that her parents came running down in a hurry.

"What happened? Is everything alright?" asked mom.

Lilly quickly showed them what she found.

"He's in Germany! Mr. Prickles is in Germany!"

Still sitting on the couch, grandma couldn't help but smile at Lilly's rejuvenated sense of joy and excitement. It was like seeing an aura of newfound hope shining out from her. Like she said, all she had to do was search.

Chapter 10

As predicted, the snowstorm ended by morning, and the airport notified Johanna that all flights had resumed. With that known, Gunther started saying his farewell to Mr. Prickles as his mom went outside to start the car.

"Me and Holland are both going to miss you, Mr. Prickles. I wish you could stay with us longer, but my mom said that you have to go back home. The good news, though, is that she said she talked to your family through the messages they sent and that they would do a video chat so we can see each other again. That means we can still be friends even though we're far away."

By his father's suggestion, Gunther went up to his room and grabbed some hedgehog treats to put in the kennel, just in case he got hungry on his long trip.

"Alright, the car is all ready and warm," said Johanna, entering from outside. "Is Mr. Prickles all set and ready to go?"

"Yes, he's ready," answered Gunther.

"Good. Then we should probably get going."

With that said, she picked up the kennel and put it on the passenger seat of her car, buckling it in for safety.

Standing at the door with Holland in his hand and his father beside him, Gunther waved goodbye as they drove away.

* * *

As soon as she arrived at the airport, Johanna reported Mr. Prickles to the person working at the customs counter. They thanked her and said that they would notify the family right away. Before leaving, Johanna looked inside the kennel one last time, saying her farewell and wishing him a merry Christmas. After that, she left to continue on with her workday.

A customs agent then came by and picked up Mr. Prickles to be registered for departure. They gathered all of his information and finally called Lilly's father to let him know that they had their pet hedgehog. Surprisingly, there remained only one flight scheduled for the United States. With it being so close to Christmas, most international flights had waned down. However, as a show of effort that he would not get lost again, the airline promised that he would not be placed in the bottom of the plane but would instead sit with the pilots. Lilly's family seemed to appreciate the nice gesture by them. With all of that done and settled, the customs agent set Mr. Prickles aside to be picked up by the pilot.

It would only take a couple minutes for the door to open and a pilot to walk in.

"Hello, I'm here to pick up the hedgehog," he explained, speaking to the agent.

"Oh, you're early. I thought the plane wasn't supposed to leave for another hour?" asked the customs agent.

"Yes, we are, but I thought it'd be better to get him as soon as I could just in case things got busy."

Upon glancing up from his kennel, Mr. Prickles suddenly realized that the pilot who stood next to him was the same one that was with Johanna the day before.

"I see, that's understandable," they said. "Well, everything is documented, and he's all ready to go."

"Great," said the pilot, grabbing onto the kennel. "I guess I'll be on my way then. Thanks again, and Merry Christmas to you."

"Merry Christmas to you too."

The pilot lifted the kennel up to his face as they walked out, looking in at Mr. Prickles.

"Hey, little guy, remember me? We met yesterday. I was with that nice lady that took you to her house."

Mr. Prickles curiously sniffed around at him through the kennel gate.

"I never got a chance to introduce myself to you. My name's Victor. Believe it or not, we're going to be flying together. Isn't that great? Who would've thought we'd ever see each other again?"

After having recognized his smell, he went on to let out a welcoming squeak.

"Yep, I think we're going to have a good time flying together. It's not often we let animals in the cockpit, but you're a special case. How does that sound?"

Mr. Prickles once again let out a squeak, followed by a smile.

With all that done, both of them made their way to the plane. Mr. Prickles was about to say bye to the kind people of Germany. He knew that he would be on his way back to Lilly and his family.

However, not everything was as it seemed. Something devious behind the scenes had been brewing. Back at the customs area where they had been at walked a woman in a pilot's uniform. She went up to the counter to talk to the agent from before.

"Hello, I'm here to pick up a hedgehog that I'm supposed to take with me. It's registered under the name Mr. Prickles," she informed them.

The customs agent immediately gave off a look of confusion.

"What do you mean? He was already picked up," they explained.

"That's not possible," she told them.

"Are you sure? It might've been the co-pilot that was here. Maybe he's on the plane. The man who—" the pilot stopped them mid-sentence.

"No, that's still impossible."

"Why?"

"Because my co-pilot is a woman."

The customs agent had no idea what to make of the situation. The unexpected turn of events left them stunned.

"But…but…oh no."

"What 'oh no?'" the pilot asked.

Unbeknownst to them and everyone else, Mr. Prickles was already up in the sky, headed to a destination that remained a mystery to all but his kidnapper, Victor.

Chapter 11

Flying in planes had become a recurring affair for Mr. Prickles. In fact, it had gotten to the point where he'd probably been on more flights than any other hedgehog in history. Enough to where he should've earned flyer miles. Who would've ever thought? But hey, at least the flights were free. Nothing could beat that deal. To make things even better, they let him sit in the cockpit. Sitting so high up front allowed him the privilege to get a front view of the sky that few got to see. Unfortunately, he ended up falling asleep soon after take-off and didn't get much chance to see any of it.

"All monitors and system routes are looking good. We should be arriving in Poland about ten minutes earlier than scheduled. That's a new record for us," explained the co-pilot.

"Good," said Victor.

Upon continuing the flight, a curious thought reentered the co-pilot's mind. Something that seemed odd and had been going through his thoughts since they had left Germany.

"So, tell me again why we have a hedgehog on board with us?" he asked.

"I don't see how it's any of your business, but I'll tell you anyway. I bought it at a pet store in Berlin to give to my daughter as a gift for Christmas," replied Victor.

"Really? I didn't know that you had a family. You're always so busy flying, I figured it was just you and this job."

"Yes, I have a family; believe it or not. Unfortunately, this job hasn't allowed me much time to spend with them. In fact, it's been nearly a month since I've been home. What can anyone expect from the busiest time of the year though? I'm just hoping that bringing this hedgehog to my daughter will help make up for my absence."

"Well, that's a good gift if you ask me. I'm sure she'll like it. Little girls always love small pets like that."

"Yes, I know it's a good gift," Victor sourly replied. "I wouldn't have gotten it if it wasn't."

"Geez, someone's in a grumpy mood today. I didn't know I was flying with Mr. Scrooge. Sorry for even asking."

"Look, I'm sorry," he apologetically said. "I've just been really stressed lately. Can we just focus on flying right now?"

"Sure," said the co-pilot.

Victor made it clear that he wasn't in much of a talkative mood, which wasn't unusual for him. He never really had the reputation of being a social person to begin with. Victor simply wanted to focus on completing the rest of the flight deliveries.

The only thing that was on his mind was getting home in time for Christmas. It was something that his family requested right before he left for his long tour of work. The family that he so seldom saw. Unfortunately, he would have to make three more stops before getting there. The odds of him arriving home before then were slim, however, and he began thinking that he would end up arriving either late at night or the day after; the same as he did the previous year and the year before that.

Victor never enjoyed letting his family down by missing Christmas. Unfortunately, his demanding job never gave him much of a choice. The company he worked for was one of the busiest in the world, and packages were expected to be shipped. It was hard work, but he did it for his wife and daughter. In fact, the only reason he stole Mr. Prickles was for them. He knew that it was wrong, but when he first saw him, he knew that it was something his daughter would love. In Victor's eyes, Mr. Prickles was less of a pet and more of a way to make things up to his daughter. Sadly, he didn't stop to consider that by doing so meant breaking another girl's heart. As with most foul deeds, his began with good intentions.

It was evening time when the plane landed down at Warsaw Chopin Airport. As usual, Victor and the co-pilot got off while the unloading crews emptied the plane of packages. With the kennel holding the sleeping Mr. Prickles hanging from his hand, Victor made his way into the airport to wait for their next scheduled departure. In the meantime, he went to look for a cafe or restaurant where he could eat at. He wasn't too familiar with Polish cuisine, though, so he ended up just getting a cheeseburger and fries at a fast-food counter. With it being so late in the day, he was pretty much the only one there. It was at this time that Mr. Prickles started waking up from his sleep. He quickly looked outside his kennel, hoping to see familiar surroundings, but soon realized that he was still far away from home.

"Well, looks like someone finally decided to wake up," said Victor.

Mr. Prickles curiously looked up at him. He then squeaked as if trying to tell him something. Unfortunately, Victor had never been around hedgehogs before him, so he was unfamiliar with their unique lingo.

"I'm sorry, I don't know what you want."

After a minute, though, Victor realized that Mr. Prickles was aiming his sniffling nose towards his food. It soon became apparent to him what he wanted.

"Are you hungry?" he asked.

Much to Victor's surprise, Mr. Prickles almost instantly shook his head.

"Wow, you sure are a smart little guy," he commented. "I knew there was something special about you when we first met. And I'm not just talking about your hat and scarf either. Here's the thing though, I don't know what hedgehogs eat. I could give you some of my food, but I don't want to risk you getting sick. I'm sorry."

Mr. Prickles finally responded with another squeak after he realized he wasn't getting anything to eat.

"What? I said I'm not giving you my food. So you're just going to have to wait."

Once again, after not getting any food, Mr. Prickles squeaked, only this time it was louder. Victor tried to ignore his pleas, but he kept on repeatedly squeaking out louder and louder. Finally, it got to the point where he couldn't take it anymore.

"Okay! Okay! I'll get you some food!" he said, setting his burger down on the table. "I'm not giving you any of this though. Just wait while I look online to see what stuff I can feed you."

Following a quick search on his phone and learning what hedgehogs ate, Victor figured out what to get him.

"Okay, I'm going to get you some food. I'll be right back. You wait here…wait. What am I saying? Where would you even go? I swear, all this flying is making me go crazy."

Feeling a little foolish, Victor soon left to get Mr. Prickles his food. It would take him a few minutes to find a place that sold one, but he eventually returned with an apple. Using a plastic knife, he cut it into little, bite-sized squares. He then carefully let Mr. Prickles out of his kennel so that he could eat freely on the table.

"Alright, here you go. Don't say I never did anything for you," he said.

Realizing that Mr. Prickles would likely get hungry again, Victor thought it best to cut up the rest of the apple and put the pieces inside of a small to-go container that he found.

While waiting for his next flight to be announced as ready-for-departure, Victor decided to try and call his family. He knew it was late at night and that they were probably sleeping, but he still tried anyway. Much to his disappointment, there was no answer. He was really hoping to talk to them, to hear their voices, but as he had learned, his job usually made that difficult.

With his phone still out, Victor got curious and searched for the Polish word for hedgehog.

"Hmm. It says here they call you a 'jezyk' in this country. That's interesting."

Mr. Prickles found it amusing that so many cultures had different names for his kind.

They both eventually finished their meals, and there was nothing left for them to do but wait until it was time to leave. As they waited, the curious hedgehog decided to observe his mysterious surroundings again. He gazed around with curious eyes. Unlike his two previous layovers, he had not been given a tour or taken to meet new people. By the way Victor talked and treated him, he knew that neither would likely happen. The fact was kind of a letdown because while he missed his home, he very much enjoyed seeing the sights of new places.

Mr. Prickles was amazed when he saw the Eiffel tower in France and the inviting people of Germany. So naturally, he wanted to see what Poland had to offer. Sadly though, that would be impossible even if he could, because a voice on the loudspeaker suddenly called for Victor, informing him that his plane was loaded and ready to leave.

Not wanting to waste a minute, Victor quickly put Mr. Prickles back in his kennel, picked it up, and made his way to the terminal. Before Mr. Prickles even knew it, they were up high in the sky again, headed to their next destination.

Chapter 12

"Guess who's feeling better and walking again?" asked grandma to her family sitting in the living room.

"Is it grandpa?" replied Lilly.

"That's right!" she said. "I present to you all the one of restored health and vigor — Grandpa!"

Everyone clapped together as the eldest man of the family came walking in with his cane. Cheers and smiles greeted him as he slowly approached.

"No need to make a parade over me," he said, making his way to the recliner. "Although, I do appreciate the loving attention. Makes me feel like I'm a movie star."

"We're just really glad to see you on your feet again," said Lilly's mom. "You had us really worried for a while."

"Worry? What's to worry about?" he asked. "I feel fine. What I had was just a little hiccup in my heart. You guys seem to forget that I was a star athlete in my youth. It's going to take a lot more than that to bring me down. This old horse still has a lot of ride left in him."

"We know you do, dad. Just try to be more careful from now on. Even amazing people like you need to wind down a little after a while."

"I know," he said. "But it doesn't mean that I can't pretend I'm young every once in a while. Besides, being young is what life is all about. Isn't that right, Lilly?" he asked, turning his attention over to his granddaughter.

"Um…I think so," she replied.

"You're supposed to say yes," he explained with a smile.

"Oh, then yes."

"Atta girl."

Having gotten comfortable in his cushioned recliner, he casually pulled the lever on the side, lifting his feet up.

"So, what happened while I was stuck in bed? Any news? I remember hearing some commotion going on around the house yesterday."

They then went on to explain everything that happened to Lilly's pet hedgehog, Mr. Prickles. From them deciding to bring him along for the trip, to him being mistakenly shipped to Paris, and him then somehow ending up in Germany, where another family with a hedgehog of their own took care of him. The whole chain of events sounded almost too unbelievable to grandpa. They then finally explained that he was being sent back to them and were just waiting for the phone call to go and pick him up.

"Wow, it sounds like your little friend went on quite the adventure," he said to Lilly. "I thought stuff like that only happened in the movies."

"Yeah, I can't wait until he gets back so I can hear all his stories."

"You know, that reminds me of a story about something that happened a long time ago to a guy I used to work with at the factory. I forgot his name, but every day he would go and…" as grandpa told another one of his long, drawn-out stories from his old job, grandma went and took Lilly with her into the kitchen to help prepare some treats for them to eat.

Lilly really enjoyed spending time with her grandma. Since they lived so far away from each other, they seldom got to do things that allowed them to connect and talk together. She was like both a second mom and friend to her. She also showed her a lot of new things too. Stuff that her own mother never had the time to since she was often so busy at work. One of the new fun things that she learned was how to knit. Grandma was a pro at knitting, and she felt one of the best things to do was teach Lilly the basics of her craft. She promised Lilly that they would make a new piece of clothing for Mr. Prickles when he returned. The idea brought some much-needed comfort to her. After all, she was still very worried about her missing hedgehog and needed to keep her mind on positive things until he found his way back home.

As they were preparing the plates and cups, a curious thought then popped into Lilly's mind. Something that she had wondered about since they first left home for her grandparent's state of Arizona.

"Grandma," she said. "Has it ever snowed here?"

"Snow? No, I'm afraid it rarely snows here. It gets a little cold like it is now, but snowfall is almost never seen here. Maybe once a decade."

"Oh," she said.

Grandma could hear the disappointment in her voice. It was obvious that while she was with family, the one ingredient of Christmas that she was used to was still missing.

"That doesn't mean it's out of the realm of possibility though," she said. "I mean, crazier things have happened. Who knows, maybe Santa will work some of his magic for us this year."

Lilly smiled. "I really hope he does."

"And don't forget. Christmas isn't only about snow and gifts. It's about being together with family," she reminded her. "If you ask me, us sitting around that brightly lit tree together and talking makes it Christmas enough. Trust me, when your little friend Mr. Prickles returns from his adventure, you'll see how it's the ones we love the most that make Christmas what it is."

Lilly once again gave off a smile.

Meanwhile, back in the living room, grandpa had just finished telling his old story to a more than patient audience.

"You never disappoint us with your crazy work stories," said Lilly's mom.

"Oh, I've got tons of them, but we'll save those for another day."

As they went on to talk about something else, Lilly's dad suddenly noticed that his phone started ringing. He instantly recognized the number as the one from the airport and quickly answered it.

"Hello? — Yes, is he ready for us to pick up?" he asked, expecting good news about Mr. Prickles.

Grandpa and Lilly's mom both shushed themselves to listen in on the conversation.

"Excuse me, what?" dad asked, thinking he misunderstood what was said.

The person on the phone regretfully informed him that their hedgehog was not at the airport and that they were once again unsure of his whereabouts.

The unwelcome news came as a shock to him. The look on his face signaled to both grandpa and mom that something was wrong.

"What? This has to be a joke. How in the world is it possible that you guys could have lost him for a third time?"

The person on the phone then clarified the situation, explaining that what had happened was different from the previous two situations.

"Wait a minute. If you didn't lose him, then what happened?" dad asked, growing impatient.

They then explained the full case of Mr. Prickles' disappearance in its entirety. All grandpa and mom could do was watch and wait.

After about a minute, Lilly's father was finally told everything. His eyes opened wide with shock as he exclaimed to the person on the phone.

"He was stolen?!"

Chapter 13

The winters in Eastern Europe were often harsher than what most people from other parts of the world would be used to, but the winters in Russia proved to be twice as harsh. Even for experienced pilots such as Victor, the unrelenting might of mother nature's freezing fury still intimidated him, as it made flying more stressful. He was just grateful that it was still daytime, as flying at night would've naturally made it doubly difficult. Another good thing was that Belarus turned out to be a quick and easy stop for him, which meant he only had two more stops on his route. After that, he could finally go home to his family. The bad thing, however, was that he had heard rumors of another blizzard approaching. The last thing he wanted was to get stranded in Russia, thus costing him more precious time. In the end, all he could do was hope for the best that everything would turn out fine.

"Looks like we should be landing in Moscow pretty soon," said the co-pilot.

"Yes, in about ten more minutes," said Victor. "Then after we're finished there, we'll be headed off to Khabarovsk, then we'll be done for the year."

"I can't wait," he said before adding: "I bet your new hedgehog can't wait either."

Hearing the co-pilot mention the connivingly acquired pet made Victor turn around and check on him. Seeing Mr. Prickles there in his deep state of sleep made him question and wonder. For a second, as he glanced at the miniature hat and scarf, he felt an unexpected sense of guilt come over him. Victor never stopped to think about the unknown family he had stolen him from. He didn't know who he belonged to or his history. The only thing on Victor's mind at the time when he snatched him up was what a great gift he would make.

Unfortunately, Victor distanced himself from his guilt and remained convinced that Mr. Prickles would be more valuable to his daughter. And in doing so, he made the decision to rip the tag bearing his name off from the kennel. No longer would people be able to identify him if they came searching. From that point forward, he would simply be a uniquely dressed hedgehog without a name.

The plane would land at Sheremetyevo International Airport without a hitch. As usual, they left the plane while the workers were busy unloading it. Once they made their way inside, Victor searched for the lounge area to wait out the majority of his stay. He knew that the layover waiting time would be longer compared to his past wait times.

Unsurprisingly, it wasn't the first time he had been in Moscow. He usually went there a dozen times a year. Although, it was always for work, never for leisure. A part of him wished he had the opportunity to see the sights as a tourist, but his busy schedule simply made that impossible. Instead, all he could do was look through the windows at the city in the far distance. He always took pictures on his phone to show his family when he returned home, as he usually did with all his arrivals.

Evening time was nearing as Victor looked down at his watch. He wanted to leave before sunset and was just eagerly waiting for his name to be paged on the loudspeaker. As he put his attention back out to the scenery outside, Victor suddenly heard a rustling sound coming from the kennel, followed by a squeak. He recognized the squeak from last time as meaning that a certain hedgehog was hungry.

"Here. This is the last of it," he said to Mr. Prickles, giving him the remaining pieces of the apple from earlier. "I'm not buying you any more food after this either. You're just going to have to wait until I take you home."

Mr. Prickles simply ignored his words as he feasted on his meal.

Not long after that, Victor noticed a group of people from a recent arrival walking past him. There were at least a few dozen people creating a commotion talking amongst themselves. He didn't understand their language, but he guessed it to be Russian from how it sounded. Families and people of all ages walked past him. Some even glanced over at Mr. Prickles, who was gobbling up his apple for all to see. Eventually, a little girl walked by and caught sight of him.

"Mama! Yozhik!" she yelled to her mother with excitement while pointing at Mr. Prickles. "Ya khochu pogladit eto."

Soon after, the mother took her daughter by the hand and led them up to Victor, as she clearly wanted to get a closer view of his hedgehog. It was obvious to him what she wanted, but he had to make it known that he didn't understand a single word of their language.

"I'm sorry, I don't speak Russian. Only English."

"Don't worry. I can tell you aren't from around here," the mother replied in a near perfect English accent. "My daughter, Natasha, noticed your hedgehog though, and she wanted to see if she could pet it."

Natasha's eyes were fixated on Mr. Prickles as he ate his apple. The way his little mouth nibbled away made her smile.

"Um…I don't know. He hasn't been out of his cage in a while and—" her mother cut him off before he could finish his denial.

"Please," she said. "It would really help to brighten her day."

Looking again at Natasha, she somewhat reminded Victor of his own daughter. He didn't want to let Mr. Prickles out in fear that he would try to run away, but he nevertheless gave in and agreed.

"Okay, but be careful. Please."

The mother then told her daughter that she could hold and pet the hedgehog but had to be careful and gentle.

Finally, Victor carefully opened the kennel door. Mr. Prickles immediately noticed and walked towards the opening. It looked like he was going to run away, as Victor had warned, but instead, he ended up walking into Natasha's hands. For whatever reason, he naturally gravitated towards her. Maybe it was because she had a friendly aura about her. Or maybe it was because she reminded him of Lilly. Whatever the case, it was apparent that they had become good friends. As she wished, Mr. Prickles let her pet him. Natasha told her mother that its hat and scarf were adorable and that she had never seen a hedgehog dressed up before. She agreed that he was very cute and unique.

"Kak yego zovut?" asked Natasha.

"She wants to know what his name is," translated her mother.

"His name…oh…um, his name is…Mr. Hedgehog," he told them.

"Privet, Mr. Hedgehog," said Natasha, saying hello.

Mr. Prickles naturally gave her a funny look at what she called him.

She kept gently holding him in her arm. However, the longer she did, the more anxious Victor got.

Natasha finally asked her mother to take a picture of them together.

"She wants me to take a picture of them together. Would that be alright?"

Victor was immediately against it. The reason being was that he knew they would most likely post the image online. He was no stranger to how social media worked, and he didn't want to risk the possibility of his owners discovering it. If they knew where he was, then they would more than likely try to trace his whereabouts. Victor simply couldn't have that, and so he denied her request to take a picture.

"I'm sorry, but I really can't let you do that."

"Why not?" asked her mother, appearing shocked by his response. "Because…because—" much to his relief, he abruptly heard his name called out from the loudspeaker, informing him that the plane was ready. "—Because we have to leave. That was my name they called for. The plane is ready, and I can't be late," he said, quickly snatching Mr. Prickles from Natasha's hands and placing him back into the kennel.

And with that, Victor was off with Mr. Prickles in his hand as the mother and daughter were left both confused and saddened by the turn of events. After all, all they wanted was to get a picture. There was no need to be so rude.

Victor ran to the terminal and got inside the plane. After a few minutes, they were finally off to Khabarovsk.

Chapter 14

"What? Somebody stole my granddaughter's pet hedgehog?" asked grandpa upon first being told the news. "You just let me know where that no-good punk thief is at, and I'll get it back. I may look old, but I've still got some fight left in me," he said, swirling his fists up in the air.

"Don't strain yourself, dad. Please," said Lilly's mom. "I know you want to help, but getting yourself all worked up isn't going to do much. Plus, there isn't anything we can do as of right now. We have no idea where Mr. Prickles is, and neither do the people at any of the airlines. All we can do for the time being is wait and hope for some good news to come in."

"I don't know what kind of cruel, heartless person could even think to steal a poor helpless hedgehog," said grandma. "And during Christmas of all things."

"I don't know either, mom. All I know is that Lilly is taking the news very hard. I didn't want to tell her, but we really couldn't let her go on without knowing. I honestly wish we had never brought him along. Then none of this would have ever happened. But when she first heard we were coming here for Christmas, she was adamant about him coming with us. Now that all this happened though…I don't know. I only hope the grief doesn't eat away at her heart."

"And no one has replied to your post online asking if he's been seen or spotted anywhere?" asked grandma.

"No. It's gotten a little over a thousand views and likes, but so far, no one has sent any clues. The only responses I've received have been well wishes and prayers from people hoping that we find him. I honestly don't know anymore. At this point, with Christmas being only a few hours away, it's going to take a miracle."

Things seemed so uncertain for them. They all felt so helpless over the unpleasant turn of events.

"Have you talked to Lilly since you told her the news?" asked grandma. "I know she was crying a lot, but maybe if we all tried to comfort her together, we might be able to get her through this pain."

"I did, but she just locked herself inside the bedroom and said that she didn't want to talk to anyone," she explained. "Fortunately, her father said he was going to try again."

"That's good. Hopefully, he can reach her this time."

"Yes, I hope so."

Over at the other part of the house in that upstairs hallway was Lilly's dad standing outside the locked bedroom. Just like the other parent, he also seemed to be very exhausted and emotional.

"Hey, kiddo…" he said, knocking softly on the door. "Can I come in? I know you're really sad right now, but in times like these, it really helps to talk to someone."

Lilly simply cried and told him that she didn't want to talk to anyone. That the only thing she wanted was to see Mr. Prickles again.

Hearing his daughter cry like that broke his heart as much as it did hers. In that moment, he wanted nothing more in the world than to take the feelings of pain and sorrow away from her. As with all fathers, he often tried to be a superhero, hoping to guard her from all despair. Sadly, his powers only went so far. For no one had the ability to instantly take away a person's sadness. Not even would-be supermen. Only patience and understanding could do that.

"Okay, I understand. You don't have to talk if you don't want to," said dad. "However, would you mind if I talked a little?"

She remained silent, and he took her silence as no objection.

"Well, this has been some crazy week, hasn't it?" he asked, pausing to let her answer, but as he expected, Lilly still chose to remain silent. "You know, this reminds me a lot of one Christmas I had when I was younger. Back when I was your age, Christmas was my favorite time of the year. Everything about it just made me so happy. The snow, the time off school, and, of course, the presents," he said through the door. "I can remember every year patiently waiting late at night for Santa to come by and deliver my presents. I would even leave him cookies and milk, just like you always do. You want to know something though?"

Dad paused again for a moment, hoping that Lilly would answer. She remained silent, however, so he continued on.

"Well, there was one Christmas where I wasn't happy. In fact, I was the opposite of happy. I was so sad that I never even bothered to open the presents I got because I knew they wouldn't bring me any joy whatsoever. Do you want to know why I was so sad that particular Christmas?" he asked, but was still left unanswered. "I was sad because my dog had passed away a few days prior. The best friend that I had known for the first sixteen years of my life. After he passed, I didn't talk to anyone because my heart was broken; much like yours is right now. I shut myself in and kept my emotions to myself. I kept them in because I thought nobody in the world would ever understand. Then one day, a random girl at school came up to me and asked why I looked so sad. She genuinely wanted to know so she could give me some support. I don't know why. Maybe I was just tired of holding everything in, but I just let it out and told her everything. Soon after, she gave me a hug, talked to me, and we naturally became great friends. Following some time together, we fell in love. Then, we got married, and finally, we had you. What I'm trying to say, Lilly, is that it never helps to shut yourself in like this. By keeping yourself shut-in, you're keeping the love of others out. I know it's hard, but it's times like these when you have to be strong. It's just like what your grandma said; you have to have hope. I can't promise you that everything is going to be alright and that Mr. Prickles will find his way back here. What I can promise you, though, is that you will always have people here for you. Whether you're happy or sad, crying or laughing, we will always be here with arms wide open."

With nothing else to say, dad simply waited there for a moment, expecting her to finally open the door. But sadly, the door remained closed. Having said all he could, he decided to head back downstairs and simply wait. However, right at the last moment, he heard the door slowly creak open. He turned, and there in the doorway stood Lilly, her face clearly ravaged by a waterfall of tears. Dad naturally held his arms open to her. It didn't even take one second for her to run into his embrace, hugging him for support.

"I'm scared, dad!" she cried. "I'm scared that I'm never going to see Mr. Prickles again."

"I know, sweetie. I know."

"He's my best friend in the world, and I need him with me again."

"I understand. Don't forget that we're worried too. He's part of our family."

Dad simply hugged her, allowing her to let out all of her emotions. There they stood together for a moment in time, comforting each other. Then, finally, he gave her a loving kiss on her forehead.

"Come on. Let's head downstairs," he said, putting his hand on her shoulder. "It's Christmas Eve, and we should be spending this time together as a family. Plus, I saw that they're playing the one Rudolph the Red-Nosed Reindeer movie that you really like. What's say we watch it together. I'm sure everyone would enjoy watching it. We can even tell Grandma to make some more cookies for us."

Lilly simply nodded her head, giving off a slight, but still much-needed smile.

They all sat and watched the movie together. It helped alleviate Lilly's worried mind for a little, but deep down inside, she was still thinking about her missing friend. About Mr. Prickles, who was still thousands of miles away on the other side of the world. Her family did all they could to comfort her. Grandma even gave her freshly baked butter cookies, but the loving warmth of them could not substitute the warmness of holding Mr. Prickles.

The movie soon ended, and everyone decided it was getting late, saying that it was time to go to bed. Lilly went upstairs to change into her pajamas and brush her teeth. She then got into bed and nestled herself underneath the sheets. As they did back home, mom sat beside her for a few minutes before saying goodnight.

"I know this hasn't been the best Christmas for you, sweetie, but it doesn't change the fact that it's still Christmas. Tomorrow will be a bright new day with plenty of gifts waiting to be opened. And knowing just what a good girl you've been, I'm sure Santa will be bringing lots of new toys."

"I don't want presents or toys," said Lilly. "The only thing I want for Christmas is Mr. Prickles to come back. I want Santa to know that I would give away all my presents for the rest of my life if it meant I could see Mr. Prickles again."

"I know you would," said mom with a loving smile. "I'm sure Mr. Prickles would do the same too."

Before getting her kiss goodnight, Lilly asked if they could make a wish together, mom agreed.

"Sure. What do you want to wish for?" she asked.

"My wish is for Santa to make sure Mr. Prickles is safe wherever he's at and for him to have a good Christmas. Even if we're not together, I still want him to be happy."

And they did just that. They wished for Mr. Prickles to have a merry Christmas.

Chapter 15

The plane was only halfway to Khabarovsk when they encountered the predicted snowstorm. The clouds were as dense and chilling as ever. To make matters even worse, it was at night. The co-pilot appeared wary about going through it, but Victor knew it was too late to turn back and that they had no other option but to go through and hope for the best.

Meanwhile, in the back behind them was a very hungry hedgehog who started a squeaking protest, demanding to be fed. Not only that, but he was also growing tired of being locked up inside his kennel. But above all, he wanted to go back home. Back home to Lilly and her family. He had had enough of traveling the world. Feeling that way, he did what a lone hedgehog could and squeaked to make his voice heard.

"Augh! Would you be quiet!" yelled Victor. "I told you before, I don't have any more food!"

Undeterred, Mr. Prickles kept on squeaking in defiance.

"You better give the little guy something fast because I'm starting to go crazy with all that noise," said the co-pilot.

"What do you want me to do? I don't have anything to feed it."

"I don't know, but you better think of something quick."

Having said that, the plane went further into the storm. And the further it went, the worse it got. It was at the point where they realized they could be in real danger. They knew that turbulence would soon be coming to haunt them. Unsurprisingly, even in the face of danger, Mr. Prickles remained adamant as ever and kept on squeaking. He squeaked louder and louder.

"That's it!" yelled Victor, with an angry look on his face.

"What are you doing" asked the co-pilot?

Without answering him, Victor grabbed the kennel holding Mr. Prickles, looked inside, and gave an angry glare.

"You better keep your little mouth shut!" he yelled, pointing his finger at Mr. Prickles. "If I hear one more squeak out of you, I'm going to—" he was quickly cut off mid-sentence when, without warning, Mr. Prickles angrily and defensively bit his finger.

"Ow!" shrieked Victor. "He bit me!"

Right as that happened, the entire plane started shaking. They had officially entered into turbulence. Forcing his attention away from the feisty hedgehog, Victor quickly retreated to his seat.

"How bad is it?" he asked the co-pilot.

"Bad."

The snow clouds in front of them appeared more violent than ever. They could barely make out anything as the windows were quickly getting covered with frost. It was a chaotic scene to behold. A truly frightening example of mother nature's fury. Even Mr. Prickles was beginning to look frightened.

Hoping to make it through, both Victor and the co-pilot held onto the controls as tightly as they could, trying to maneuver through the storm. They crazily pushed on forward for a few minutes, but for them, it felt like an eternity.

Then suddenly, for seemingly no reason whatsoever, the co-pilot's eyes closed, and he soon slumped to the back of his chair into unconsciousness. It was as if a sleeping spell had been cast over him.

"Hey, what's wrong?! Wake up!" shouted Victor, snapping his fingers in front of his face.

Unfortunately, no matter what he did, he wouldn't wake up. So the plane was left for a single pilot to control.

It was at that point when Victor saw something he couldn't believe. To his astonishment, all of the clouds began to part away from the middle until they dissipated away completely, leaving only the clear night sky in front of him.

"What in the world..." he muttered to himself.

From behind, Mr. Prickles appeared to be just as amazed over what happened.

Having regained smooth control over the plane again, Victor then noticed something peculiar in the distance. What he saw was a faint red dot shining in the night sky. At first, he thought it to be a star, but that was until he noticed it was getting brighter and closer. Then before he knew it, the red light swiftly flashed in front of the plane. It went so fast that he couldn't tell for sure, but it looked like it was pulling something behind. As if it were leading something. If that wasn't enough to weird Victor out, he soon heard the unexpected sound of bells jingling. Then the sound suddenly stopped. A good minute went by with nothing else, and so he thought it was all just his imagination, but that was until the most startling thing happened. From the cockpit door came a knock.

Taken by surprise, Victor jumped in his seat. No one else should have been on the plane. He peered over to the co-pilot and saw that he was still unconscious. He then turned to Mr. Prickles, who just stared at him through the kennel.

A knock sounded once again.

"Who…who's there?" he asked, sounding startled.

A voice replied. "An old friend."

"An old friend?" Victor muttered to himself.

"May I come in?" asked the mysterious visitor.

Victor was hesitant to answer. In all honesty, he quite well thought he was losing his mind. No one should have been on a plane full of delivery cargo. And yet, somebody was asking him if they could enter the cockpit.

"Sure," he timidly answered.

The door then opened, and there in the entryway stood an elderly, larger-sized man wearing a bright red and white suit and matching hat. The famous outfit, along with the black boots and white gloves, would've been enough for anyone to instantly recognize him, but it was the white beard on his face that finally relayed to Victor, the identity of the man.

"Thank you," said Santa.

Victor remained silent for a moment, not able to fathom the event that was happening. He kept on rubbing his hands over his eyes in disbelief, but the man in the bright red suit was still standing there.

"Yep, that's the reaction I always get when people your age first see me."

"What's going on? Is this a prank? A trick or something?"

"Nope. There's no trick. I promise you."

Victor still looked shocked. "You're not supposed to be real though. You can't be real."

"Why can't I be real?" Santa asked, almost sounding offended by his remark. "Touch me. Go ahead, touch me. Then you'll see that I'm as real as you."

Victor did as he was instructed and put his hand on Santa's arm. He moved his fingers over the warm, perfectly woven fabric. He couldn't believe it. True to his words, he was real.

"Why are you here? What do you want?"

"I'm here for him," said Santa, pointing to Mr. Prickles, who was still inside his kennel peering out with curious eyes.

"The hedgehog?"

"The hedgehog has a name," said Santa. "It's Mr. Prickles, remember?"

"Yes, sorry. Mr. Prickles. But what do you want him for?"

"I need to take him back home?"

"Take him home! But you can't. I need him," Victor said in protest.

"No, you don't," Santa argued. "I know you think you do, but you don't."

Victor put himself between Santa and Mr. Prickles. He looked desperate, as he truly did not want to let him go.

"You don't understand. He's supposed to be a gift for my daughter," he explained. "This is going to be the third Christmas in a row that I've missed. I've let my family down so many times by working this unbearable job; I just want to give them something to make up for being gone. Something to remind them that I still love them. Something to make them smile again."

Santa knew Victor wasn't a bad guy. Yes, he wrongfully stole Mr. Prickles, but it was clear his will was not to cause harm or do evil. He was just desperate. People in desperate times have always done regrettable things. However, it never meant that they were inherently bad people.

"He's not yours though. He belongs to another girl."

"But if you take him, then what am I going to give—" Santa cut him off before he could finish.

"Your daughter doesn't need any more gifts. She has enough to last her a lifetime. What she needs now is for you to be home for Christmas."

"How can I get home though?" asked Victor. "I still have an entire load of package cargo to deliver. There's no way I can make it home by Christmas at this point. It's too late."

"No, it's not," replied Santa. "Look in the back."

Curious to what he was talking about, Victor moved over and peered into the back of the plane. To his astonishment, the cargo area was empty. All the boxes meant to be delivered to Khabarovsk were gone.

"What?!...How?!"

"I put them all in my bag," Santa answered. "Don't worry, for me, it'll only take a few extra minutes to deliver them. Especially when I have such magnificent help like Rudolph."

"Ru...Rudolph?" asked victor.

"Yes, he's right over there," said Santa, pointing out through the window.

To Victor's shock, there he was, along with all the other reindeer, soaring the sky as they kept pace with the plane.

With everything said and done, Santa finally convinced Victor to hand Mr. Prickles over to him.

"You can go home now," he told Victor. "By my estimate, you should get there right at the break of dawn. That's plenty of time to surprise your daughter for Christmas."

Santa followed that by saying his goodbye. However, before he could leave, Mr. Prickles unexpectedly squeaked. Santa lifted the kennel up to his ear and listened. He nodded his head in an 'okay' motion.

"Mr. Prickles wanted me to tell you that he's sorry for biting you earlier," Santa explained. "He said that he didn't mean to hurt you. He was just really hungry."

Victor smiled. "It's okay. Don't worry about it." He then asked, "Um…can you tell him I'm sorry for stealing him and keeping him away from his family for so long?"

Santa did as he requested and let out a couple of similarly sounding hedgehog squeaks.

"He said he forgives you."

Victor and Mr. Prickles then both shared a hearty smile together.

"Merry Christmas," said Santa.

"Merry Christmas to you too…and to Mr. Prickles," said Victor.

And with that, Santa closed the cockpit door and left.

Within a second, Victor turned his attention out the window and saw Santa on his sleigh. They both waved bye to each other one last time as he flew away into the sky.

Soon after, the co-pilot suddenly awoke from his unexpected slumber.

"Ugh, what happened? Did I fall asleep?" he asked, seemingly confused.

"Yes, but it's alright. We've had a long night."

The co-pilot then realized that Victor was suddenly changing course away from Khabarovsk.

"Hey, why are we turning that way?"

Victor smiled. "Because we're going home."

Chapter 16

It was now midnight as the hour hand reached the twelve on the clock. Christmas day had officially arrived, but as expected, everyone was lost in their usual deep slumber. Well, everyone except for Lilly. She had been unable to fall asleep. Instead, she just lay on her bed, staring out the window at the night sky, towards the endless array of shimmering stars above her. While gazing at them, she wondered if Mr. Prickles was also looking up at them as she was. She knew that just because they were separated, it didn't change the fact that they were still under the same night sky. She believed the moon and the stars to be their one remaining connection to each other. The twinkling magic that bound their hearts together.

As another hour passed, Lilly began fluttering her eyes, signaling that she was starting to fall asleep. Little by little, she was looking to be on her way into the dream realm. Right before completely shutting her eyes, however, she suddenly heard an unexpected noise come from downstairs. It was almost like a rustling as if someone were trying to go unnoticed.

Whoever or whatever it was had nevertheless caught her attention, forcing her out of bed.

Lilly curiously looked to the room that her parents were sleeping in and to her grandparent's room, but both doors were closed. She knew then that it wasn't any of them. While walking further down the hallway, she heard the sound once again. Lilly was now convinced that an unknown stranger had entered the house. Although, for some odd reason, she found herself not feeling scared. Even though a stranger was in the house, she did not sense an unkind presence. In fact, it seemed to be the opposite, almost friendly in a way.

As she made her way down the stairs and into the living room, Lilly caught sight of a silhouette rummaging around the Christmas tree. She thought she was dreaming at first and rubbed her eyes, but the figure was still there.

"Hello?" she asked.

The figure replied, "Merry Christmas, Lilly."

Lilly finally turned on the light to see who it was, but the figure had vanished, as if never having been there at all. Instead, all she discovered were a bunch of neatly wrapped presents placed underneath the Christmas tree.

"Santa…?" she murmured, realizing who it must've been.

Not even a second later, Lilly heard a familiar sound come from underneath the tree. It was a squeak. But not just any squeak, it was a hedgehog squeak. A squeak which belonged to only one special hedgehog.

Quickly tearing the wrapping paper off, Lilly unveiled her long lost Mr. Prickles. She excitedly opened the kennel, and he immediately ran into her arms.

"It's really you!" she said with joy, holding him in her hands and kissing his little forehead. "I missed you so much!"

Mr. Prickles squeaked back in reply. She naturally knew what he was saying simply by the way his squeak sounded.

Lilly then saw something out of the corner of her eye, quickly ran to the nearest window, and looked up at the sky. In the backdrop of the glistening stars, she caught a glimpse of a sleigh being led by a group of flying reindeer. To the front of it shined a bright red light. Seeing that confirmed her suspicion of who had delivered her lost friend, and she naturally gave off a smile.

Not able to wait for another second, Lilly excitedly ran upstairs to wake everyone up and tell them the great news.

"Mom! Dad! Wake up!" she yelled as she entered their room. "Mr. Prickles is home! Santa brought back Mr. Prickles!!"

"What?" asked dad, still half asleep.

"What are you talking about, Lilly?" asked mom.

"Look!" she said, holding out Mr. Prickles to their faces.

Both of their mouths instantly dropped.

"What…how?" said dad.

"Oh my god," said mom.

Grandma and grandpa then walked into the room, clearly woken up by all the commotion.

"What's wrong? What happened?" asked grandma.

"Look for yourself," replied Lilly's mom.

Both grandparents looked at Mr. Prickles resting in Lilly's hand. They displayed the same dropped expressions of shock that her parents had.

"How?" asked grandma.

"Santa brought him home!" answered Lilly.

None of them could believe it, and yet, there was Mr. Prickles in front of them.

"Of all the things I've seen in my years alive, this one takes the cake," grandpa told them.

And if that wasn't wild enough, what dad saw when he looked out the window made things even more unbelievable.

"I don't believe it," he said.

"What?" asked mom.

"Look outside."

They looked, and what they saw amazed them. Snow was falling from the sky. Snow in the state of Arizona, where grandma said it rarely ever snowed at all.

Lilly simply smiled with awe. "This is the best Christmas ever."

She lifted Mr. Prickles up to the window and showed him all the falling snow, turning everything white. After that, everyone just stayed quiet and marveled at the magnificent sight. It was a Christmas like none other. One that Lilly and Mr. Prickles would surely remember forever.

Chapter 17

Everything on the end block of Waterbury Street was as normal as it could be for a breezy January evening. No different than any other street block. Everything was still covered with snow, a few houses still had their Christmas decorations up, and a certain family had just returned home from their trip to Arizona. Suffice to say, all was well and normal. Well, except for the fact that Mr. Prickles had become an internet celebrity almost overnight. Although, that was to be expected after Lilly and her parents posted the story of his adventure online.

"Wow, can you believe how many comments and messages we've got about Mr. Prickles?" said Lilly as her family entered their house.

"I know, our little guy is famous," replied mom.

"Hey, maybe they'll end up making a movie about him someday," said dad.

Lilly's face lit up at the idea. "That would be so cool!"

"They really should make a movie out of the Christmas we had," said mom. "I mean, it was all just one surprise after the other. Seriously. First, we left home at the last minute. Then, Mr. Prickles got lost and went on his adventure. Then, he somehow magically returned to us. And then, he gets famous. Finally, to top it all off, I found out that my company is letting me work entirely from home from now on too. I mean, how many more surprises can one family get?"

"I've got to say, learning that you're going to be with us more from now on is hands down the best Christmas gift I've received," said dad with a loving smile.

Naturally, mom gave a similarly loving smile back.

As Lilly's parents readjusted themselves and put all of their luggage and belongings away, she decided to go up to her room, where she released Mr. Prickles from his kennel. Upon exiting the enclosure, he excitedly set eyes on his familiar house and food bowl waiting there for him. With nothing restraining him, he quickly ran towards it. To be back home within his familiar surroundings was like a dream come true. Primarily because there was a point in his adventure where he thought he would never see it again. Fortunately, those worries were long in the past.

"Once you're done eating, we'll tell mom to see if we can video chat with all the friends you made," said Lilly as he ate.

"First, we'll call Stefan and Charlotte. Then after that, we'll call Gunther, so you can say hi to Holland. Finally, we'll call that one Russian girl, Natasha, who said she met you at the airport."

Mr. Prickles couldn't wait, so he started gobbling up his food, as he was looking forward to saying hello to all the friendly people he met while in Europe.

As soon as he finished eating and had a drink of water, Lilly lifted him into her arms, and they went back downstairs, where her mom set up the video calls.

First on the list were Stefan and Charlotte. Mom turned on the laptop and they both soon appeared on screen, the Eiffel Tower visibly standing behind them.

"Bonjour, Mr. Prickles," greeted Charlotte as Stefan smiled and waved. "We're so glad to see that you finally made it back home safe." They talked for a couple minutes more before finally saying, "We wish you all well and hope to see Mr. Prickles again someday." They all then waved bye to each other.

Next up came Gunther and his family. Following a short wait to connect, the familiar German family soon appeared on the screen.

"Greetings from Berlin!" said Johanna with a smile.

"Guten tag!" said Lilly in her best attempted German accent.

"Guten tag!" replied Gunther, holding Holland in his hands.

"Say guten tag, Mr. Prickles," pointing his attention to the other hedgehog.

As expected, Mr. Prickles let out a friendly squeak. Holland did likewise.

They then talked for a few minutes before wishing each other well and saying their goodbyes.

Finally, the last on their list was Natasha, the young girl from Moscow, who said she had met Mr. Prickles at the airport.

They messaged her, and soon enough, she and her mother appeared on the screen.

"Privet, Mr. Hedgehog," greeted Natasha.

Natasha's mother then whispered into her ear, appearing to explain something. She soon nodded her head, understanding the correction.

"Oh! Privet, Mr. Prickles!"

Not having the chance to get a picture of him while they met at the Moscow airport, Natasha asked her mother if she could take a screenshot of him. Lilly and her mom both agreed and held Mr. Prickles to the camera.

"Say cheese!" said Natasha's mother.

Asked expected from such a unique and friendly hedgehog, Mr. Prickles looked at them and smiled.

They all ended up talking for a little while before finally wishing each other well and saying their goodbyes.

After having finished reconnecting Mr. Prickles with his old friends, Lilly's mom explained it was getting late and that she should start getting ready for bed.

However, before she did so, an unexpected message soon appeared on the screen. It was from an unknown sender, but they made it known that they loved Mr. Prickles and wanted to see if they could ask Lilly a few questions on video chat.

Lilly asked her mom if it was alright, and she agreed.

On the screen appeared a girl close to the same age as Lilly. She introduced herself as Tina. They talked for a couple of minutes until she revealed that she had recently received a hedgehog as a gift and was wondering where they got Mr. Prickles his hat and scarf. Tina said that she wanted to get similar ones for her hedgehog. Lilly and her mom told her. They then asked if they could see her hedgehog. She said that her dad was holding it but asked him to come over and say hi. Soon, a man appeared on the screen. Lilly and her mom both greeted her father and told him that their hedgehog was adorable.

While Tina's father was a brand-new face to them, his identity was all too familiar to Mr. Prickles. Why? Because Tina's father just so happened to be Victor, the pilot who had 'borrowed' him and taken him through most of Europe. However, on closer inspection, Mr. Prickles noticed that he wasn't in his pilot's uniform. Instead, he wore a different kind of work uniform, signaling that he had changed careers.

"Thank you for giving my lovely daughter here the chance to ask her question. She's been so excited about her new prickly friend ever since I brought him home yesterday," said Victor.

"That's so sweet," said Lilly's mom. "Tell me, what made you decide on getting a hedgehog anyway? I've learned that every family has their own unique story."

Victor turned his attention to Mr. Prickles and smiled. "Well, I guess you could say I was inspired by some events that happened over Christmas. Also, I've kind of taken a liking to these prickly, little critters. They really do make good pets. But more importantly, they make great friends."

"Yes, they certainly do," said Lilly as she snuggled Mr. Prickles in her arms.

"Well, we should get going," said Victor. "It's getting late, and we need to go to bed soon. However, for our hedgehog, his night is just starting."

"Hey, maybe we can visit you someday so our hedgehogs can have a playdate together," said Lily

Victor smiled at the idea, and so did his daughter.

"Yes, that would be nice."

And with that, Mr. Prickles let out a happy squeak.

The End

Made in United States
Orlando, FL
09 December 2021

11394240R00079